The
PLAYMAKER

The
PLAYMAKER

A Chesterboro University Novel

JOSIE BLAKE

Content edits provided by Jessica Ruddick.

Line editing suggestions and initial proof provided by Red Adept Editing.

Second proofing provided by Amy Brantley.

ISBN: 978-1-955887-05-2

Contents

For every survivor.
And for my husband and boys, always.

Playmaker

(noun) a player whose role is to create scoring opportunities for his or her teammates.

Ivy

Fourteen months ago...

SHOTS MAKE COLLEGE PARTIES smell better.

I tilt my head up, letting my long curly hair fall down my back, and close my eyes. The music flows through me as I dance, the bass thumping along with my heartbeat. Laughing, I move to the rhythm. As a dance major, I've been dancing since I could stand, but wiggling my body along with the rest of the sweaty, euphoric people in the room differs from dancing on stage. No one is watching me here. Right now, I don't have to be no-nonsense, overachieving Ivy Deveraux, destined for performing. Tonight, I only want to be Ivy Deveraux, regular drunk college girl at a party.

I'll return to responsibility tomorrow, though thoughts of what waits there make me need another drink. I motion to the three girls I'm with—other girls in my major. They nod or give me a thumbs up but stay to dance. I grin as I shimmy toward the bar. Not too much pulls me away from a dance floor.

At the bar, a guy wearing a Chesterboro Bulldogs hockey T-shirt pours me a beer from a keg in a trash can full of ice. Even though I'm swaying on my feet, I pay close attention while he works. My dad harped on me about what happens to girls at parties when they take their eyes off their drinks. Satisfied that hockey guy hasn't roofied me, I tip the Solo cup back and gulp down half of the contents. Beer is nasty, so I take it like medicine—as quickly as possible. Besides, the music calls me back to the dance floor.

I pause for a breath, wincing. Seriously, the stuff is disgusting. Bringing the cup back to my lips, I steady myself to finish it.

"Pinching your nose helps too." As I power through my drink, chugging it down, I shift so I can make eye contact with the newcomer. But then I need to tilt my head up—and up—until I meet a pair of sharp brown eyes. I sway, but I don't blame the drink. Instead, I suspect it's the impact from all that gorgeous guy-ness and his too-discerning gaze.

Not sure what to say, I polish off the cheap beer then put the empty cup on the bar, where it promptly falls over. I right it and wrinkle my nose as the carbonation burns. "Yuck."

He chuckles, and the sound sends heat through me. Cocking my head, I take in my companion. He's definitely over six feet and covered in muscles with wide shoulders and trim hips— he's in great shape. He wears a black T-shirt, and tattoos snake along his forearms, disappearing under his sleeves. He leans against the bar with one foot up on the chair next to me, and the curve of his butt and thighs is aesthetic perfection. I'm a dancer—I can't help but admire hips and legs like those.

It's his eyes that draw me, though. Even four shots and a chugged beer in, I recognize the intelligence in them. Something more than that, though, catches me, something raw and almost wild. Whatever it is, it makes my breath come shorter and my stomach flutter. "Hi."

"Hi." His lips settle into a lazy grin. "I'm Declan Mitchell." I can only blink. I spend most of my time in the studio or my room, studying, but even I recognize his name. He's on the top line of the hockey team… and is a notorious campus playboy.

He holds out his hand to me, and his eyes are heavy-lidded and sexy. Leaning down so he can put his mouth near my ear, he says, "I saw you dancing." His breath is on my cheek, and a shiver skips down my spine.

I gather myself. "That's the line you're leading with?" As a pickup, it shouldn't work for him, but I admit, it totally does.

He nods, then steps closer, curving his hands around my elbows. "The way you dance makes me want to dance with you." It's hot in the basement of Shepherd Hall, especially when packed with bodies, but I swear I can feel his body heat. I suck in a breath, but all I catch is him, a scent that's woodsy and rough.

Everything about this guy screams danger. He's obviously hot, with all those muscles and tattoos. I never expected that tattoos would be my thing, but whatever Declan is seems to be my thing. It's not only how he looks, though—it's his gaze. It's raw and tempting, as if he's daring me to say no.

I should. This is exactly the kind of guy a good girl stays away from. Except I don't want to be a good girl right now. Tonight, I don't want to think. I just want to feel alive.

I grip his tattooed forearms and lean close enough to say, "You're in luck, then. I'm on my way back out." I don't know if it's beer muscles that have me holding his gaze or whatever magnetic pull he has, but it doesn't matter. One corner of his mouth turns up. He slides his hand around to the small of my back and leads me back to the dancing.

I don't expect much. He's a hockey player, so definitely athletic. Probably graceful, too, because it takes a lot of balance to do what they do on skates. But dancing with Declan isn't like anything I've ever experienced before.

First, he's bigger than anyone I've ever danced with. I'm not short—about five-six—but most male dancers aren't usually built like he is, all rangy limbs covered in bulk. Most surprisingly, he seems to read my thoughts, anticipating how I'm going to move even before I do it. The way we sync, our bodies twining together, is electric.

Granted, the beer I just chugged is definitely going to my head. I don't drink much. I dance, so my body has always been a temple. That thought strikes me funny, and I giggle. Declan's brow tilts in question. I wave him off. Not talking about that tonight. That I'm even thinking about it means I should have another drink.

Declan leans closer. His hands are on my waist, and even though everything is fuzzy, I'm sure that feels amazing. "Do you want to go somewhere quieter?"

Do I? "Yes. Absolutely."

He winks at me and snags my hand, running his thumb over my knuckles in a way that sends tingles up my arm. He leads me, but it's way easier for him to get through the crowd than it is for me. Not only is he huge, which helps move bodies, but the other hockey players step aside for him, giving him head nods as we pass. I add their respect to what I already know about Declan. Which means I know two things—he's a playboy, and his teammates like him.

I wave at the girls I came with, motioning that I'll be right back. Their scowls say they disagree with my life choices, and Amber even shakes her head. But they don't get it. Tomorrow, this will all be gone. Tonight, I'm not saying no to anything.

I stumble, trying to keep up with Declan's longer strides, which stops him. "Sorry." He loops his arm over my shoulder, grinning. "Rushing. Come on." He guides me toward the stairs and lets me go ahead. I have no idea where we're going, though, so I step to the side at the top, and he takes the lead again. We go up another flight, and it gets quieter. Most of the doors are closed, but Declan stops in front of one and opens it, motioning me inside. It's empty.

Alone with him, nerves leak through my buzz. "Is this your room?"

He shakes his head. "No. It's Hunter's. He's manning the bar. Said I could use it."

It takes a herculean leap for my alcohol-laced brain to process that he probably cleared that with Hunter before the party began. I didn't see him talk to anyone while he was with me. "You arranged a hookup room."

His throat works as he shifts his weight. This is the first time he's looked anything less than comfortable. He shakes his head. "My friend, Linc. He's out for the season, maybe longer. Concussion. Just like that... fast, unexpected. It could have been any of us. I thought I might just want to be alone."

I wrinkle my nose. "You aren't alone, though."

"I know." He shrugs.

In the three weeks since the doctors said they suspect cancer, I've thought I wanted to be alone, but really, I only want to be away from people who didn't understand. I nod at him and squeeze his hand. I get it.

Then again, that sounds romantic, and he could have just said all that to get in my pants. Either way, he doesn't want to talk right now, and neither do I. I'm living in the moment, and as I meet Declan's gaze, I get the impression that's where he'd prefer to stay as well. I need someone who's not thinking about tomorrow, either.

I step closer to him, tentatively running my fingers up his arms as I trace the tattoos there. To see more of them, I reach for the hem of his shirt. Pausing, I meet his eyes again, and he blows me a kiss, raising his arms over his head.

I grin, pulling the shirt up and off him. His chest is magnificent, and the ink covers both of his arms and his shoulders. There isn't a lot of light in here, so I can't make out all the details, but I trace across the lines and tweak the nipple ring on his right side. He sucks in a breath that sends a wave of longing through me.

"Did that hurt?"

"A little."

I only have one hole in each ear, and I don't remember getting them, so I wouldn't know, but I nod anyway. When he reaches for my hem, I cover his fingers, except I don't want him to stop. It irritates me that I paused, so I pull the shirt over my head in one quick flick. As the cool air hits my skin, I sigh with pleasure. It was so hot downstairs.

I'm a dancer, and I wear skimpy or tight outfits all the time. I've never been self-conscious about my body, but I'm half naked in front of one of the biggest players at Chesterboro University. I resist the urge to squirm under his gaze.

But Declan's eyes are on the base of my neck. He draws one finger along it, and I cringe. "Did that hurt?" he asks, mirroring my question.

It's my still-angry biopsy scar. My heart picks up, but I wave my hand. "That's nothing."

His brow drops, and his too-sharp, skeptical gaze finds mine. I scowl back at him. *Damn it.* The scar is a perfect line, and there are still marks where the stitches were removed a few days ago. This is why I wore a high-neck shirt. I don't want people to look at it. I stop myself from reaching for my shirt and running out of here. I came into this room to make out with a hot boy, to forget that I'm sick and to feel normal again, not to be reminded about everything waiting for me in the morning.

I brace myself for the questions, but none come. Instead, he nods and drops his head. Slowly, he places the softest kiss below the scar.

Nothing could have disarmed me more completely. To my horror, my eyes sting. *Absolutely not.* I don't care if I'm half drunk. There's no way I'm crying in front of Declan and his perfect, healthy body. I snag my shirt off the ground. "This is a mistake. I should get home."

I struggle into the shirt like I'm putting on body armor. As I make for the door, my face on fire, he catches my hand. "Stay," he demands, and I stop at the authority in his voice in spite of myself.

I inhale a steadying breath. If I leave now, I'll look scared, and I'm not scared. I've been telling myself that for weeks.

I spin on him, my head high. He's still holding my hand. I tilt my head up and glare at him. "Why?"

"I want to hold you." He makes the request with the arrogance of someone who usually gets what he wants.

Out of spite, I consider denying him, just to see what he'll do. Except my body wants what he does, so I stay still, at war with myself.

Finally, he adds, "Please."

My resistance crumbles. Maybe it's the drinks that weaken me, or it could be the uncertainty hanging over my future, but I nod and allow him to tug me toward the bed in the corner. Never letting go of my hand, he stretches out on his side and tugs me down to him. I curl into his body and let him be the big spoon. He's a massive bulk behind me, his body all warm muscles. I'm thin, almost painfully so. Not only because I'm a dancer, but I've lost weight these past weeks—weight that I can't afford to lose. We shouldn't fit together, but we do. I can feel the hard press of him against the base of my spine.

He wants me, at least his body does. He only pulls me against him, though. I expect his hands or his mouth to roam, but he only holds me, as he promised.

I pinch my eyes closed. Tonight, I wanted to let loose. I wanted to forget that I don't hook up with random guys—that I don't hook up at all. Instead, somehow, I'm snuggling one of the sluttiest guys on campus, with no hookup in sight.

My lack of game is pathetic.

I can't make myself leave, though. Being pressed against him feels… perfect. With his arms around me, I don't feel like I'm going to fall apart. I feel like he's holding me together. I curl in on myself and let him shield me.

I fall asleep.

I don't know how much later it is when I wake up, but I'm warm, and there's a dull ache in my head. Behind me, Declan breathes slowly and steadily, still sleeping. I close my eyes and allow embarrassment to wash over me. I need to get out of here.

As softly as I can, I shift out of his grasp and move to stand.

"Running away?"

His voice makes me jump. "Holy crap, you scared me." I scowl down at him, but he only smiles up at me, propping his head on his elbow.

"You plan to walk of shame out of here?"

"Not shame." I shrug. "More like walk of minor awkwardness."

"Awkward?" He cocks his head. "Why?"

"We…" I wave over the bed. "Cuddled. That's sad."

"Why?" He looks confused.

I tuck my hands on my hips. "When's the last time you cuddled with someone?"

He wrinkles his nose and doesn't say anything.

"Exactly."

He shrugs. "Whatever. That's what we wanted to do, so that's what we did."

I throw my hands up and head for the door. This is too weird.

"Wait," he calls, and I stop. "I didn't even get your name."

"That's sad, too, isn't it?" I open the door to step out.

"Please."

I can't resist this guy when he says please. I sigh. "It's Ivy. My name is Ivy."

"Nice to meet you, Ivy."

I shake my head, chuckling, then slip out of the room and head downstairs. But when I'm out on the street, I realize I don't have anywhere I want to be. My phone says it's almost dawn. I don't want to go back to my room, so I start walking. The blocks fade away until the sun is fully up, and I find myself at Big Perks, the coffee shop on Hanover.

I go in and order a latte. I rarely consume dairy, but with what I'm about to go through, I doubt the empty calories matter.

At breakfast time, I get texts from the girls I went to the party with, asking if I'm okay. I'm not, but I say I am. I head to meet them at the cafeteria for food, but I don't eat anything. Eventually, I end up back in my room and sleep through most of the afternoon in fits and starts.

At four o'clock, my phone dings with a message from my mother: *When are you leaving?*

Half an hour, I reply, then drag myself from my bed, strip the sheets, and throw them into a plastic trash bag. There's nothing left in my room. I packed it all up yesterday before the party at Shepherd. All I have is an overnight bag with my necessities. I grab my toiletries and head for the shower.

Twenty-seven minutes later, I lug the bag downstairs, the trash bag full of linens over my shoulder. It's Sunday, so most people are getting ready to start another school week. Not me. I'm on my way home. I throw my bags into the back of my Honda, then slam the trunk closed.

Glancing around, I wonder if I'll be back. The quad is in front of me, practically empty, and I already miss it. Feeling foolish, I trudge around to the driver's seat and slide in. I take a deep breath as I start the car and ease out of the on-street parking spot, heading home.

Declan

The Present...

"A DANCE COMPETITION?" I drop the flyer on Coach's desk and push it back toward him. "Is this a joke?"

Coach Chandler leans back in his chair, running a hand over his face. "Mitch, listen... it's a fundraiser."

"Can't we sell magazines or something? Cookies?" I open my arms wide. "A wet T-shirt contest? I look amazing wet."

"God save me," he mutters. "It's not our fundraiser. It's the performing arts department's. They're raising money to make improvements to their main theater. A sort of Dancing with the Stars style show."

"And the athletes are the stars?" This is a nightmare. When the team voted me captain, I never expected this.

"It's not only athletes. They want campus leaders. Fraternity and sorority presidents, the head of student government... and the captains of the sports teams."

I stand up, pacing. "I don't dance like that, Coach. Sure, I can shake my ass at the bar, but this?" I snap my fingers. "You know who's good at this? Linc. He can dance. We should ask him." Linc is one of my assistant captains. He would hate me throwing him under the bus like this, but everyone likes him. He'd be a great face of our team for this thing.

Coach shakes his head. "Reynolds is out with a groin injury. You know how that stuff goes. He needs to be focused on rehab, not some publicity stunt. The organizers want to start practicing for this thing next week."

He's right. Linc got hurt a couple of weeks ago, the weekend before Thanksgiving. His rehab is going well, but he's in a weird place. Maybe it's because he'd only been back on the ice for a month or so after being out for almost a year before that with concussions. I tried to talk to him, but he blew me off. I wonder if it has something to do with Shea Carmichael, a friend of his from home. They're avoiding each other. She even texted me instead of Linc to get some guys together to help her on a Habitat for Humanity project this weekend.

Definitely suspicious, but Linc said he was going to handle it. No idea what that means. It's not my biggest problem right now.

I search for other options. "Griff..." Griffin Parker is another of my roommates and my other assistant captain. He works out at a mixed martial arts gym. I've seen him be graceful in a cage while he kicked someone's ass.

"You're the captain, Mitch. It's got to be you."

Shit. I fall back into the seat in front of his desk with a sigh. "I know."

I wanted the captain letter this year and had done everything short of actively campaigning to get it. After our team lost in the championship game last spring, all the talking heads went on and on about how my impulsiveness on the ice could have contributed. I'll admit to taking a couple of ill-fated chances in that game. But our team needed a spark in the third period, something to get us going. The risks hadn't worked, though, and one disastrous play had even ended up in our opponent's net.

Something like that is forgivable in a regular-season game or when you're up on the scoreboard, but not when the score is tied, and the championship is on the line.

What followed was a summer of speculation about whether I'm cut out for the NHL. They called me a lone wolf and a wild card—all charisma and no substance. A hedonist with no leadership qualities. I kind of admire that assessment. The hedonist part, anyway. Good word.

Sports commentators are full of shit, but my agent believes that if I want a chance at being signed as a free agent after graduation, I need to start caring about what they say.

This year, he suggested I tone down my extra-curricular activities—namely anything fun. Fewer girls, less booze, less showing up in campus gossip. That's not a huge deal. Sure, I was pretty wild as a freshman and sophomore, but I've slowed down. Some, anyway.

The second part was the hard part. He said I need to take on a leadership role and prove that I've matured. He said assistant captain would be fine, but captain would be better.

I'm still surprised by it. Me, captain of the team.

Last year, Cord Spellman was the captain. He's the poster boy for leadership qualities, steady, calm under pressure, everyone's go-to guy. Our team loved him. Cord was an amazing captain.

I'm nothing like him.

Still, I managed what my agent asked. The team likes me. A lot of the guys even look up to me, probably because of the reputation. So far, all being captain has meant is that I need to keep an eye on the rookies when they get out of hand at parties. Easy enough.

But a dance competition is above and beyond the call of duty.

Coach sighs, leaning back in his chair. "The other big-money teams on campus are already in. Football, basketball, soccer... they even got the captain of the track team on board."

"Football?" I cock my head. "Who's their guy?"

Coach waves me off. "Who do you think? Ellison."

I smother my grin. I don't know much about Roman Ellison, but he's a huge fuckboy, maybe worse than I was. I bet he's as excited about doing this as I am. "What about classes?"

Coach picks up another paper. "Says here that the practices will start after finals. They'll pick the partners this weekend and can schedule practices next week before campus closes for holiday break. Says that they will give participants special permission to stay in student housing if they need it." He tosses the page on top of his already messy desk. "Not relevant for you, because we have a game next weekend, and you were already going to be here."

"Pick the partners?"

He shrugs. "I guess they're going to pair you up with someone from the performing arts department. A dancer. You'll perform in the show with them." I pick up the paper he discarded and read the list of names. I'm a senior and know a lot of the people on campus, so some names are familiar. But one of them catches my eye.

"Ivy Deveraux." I glance up at Coach, pointing at her name. He shakes his head and shrugs. *Right. How would he know her? But Ivy isn't a common name. Is it the same girl from a year ago?*

Her name and memory tug at me. It was the night Linc got knocked out cold on the ice. Watching how fast things changed for him… it sent me reeling. I hadn't wanted to be alone that night, but I hadn't wanted to be with people either.

I'd seen a girl dancing at the after-game party—Ivy—and there was an edge about her. Something desperate, untamed. She'd been there with a few other girls but was somehow apart from them. Even now, that doesn't make sense, but I can't deny that it had drawn me to her. I thought we were going to hook up. Except when we were alone, it was like neither of us wanted to. No, that's not right… I definitely wanted to. But we didn't. Instead, we curled up together on Hunter's bed and fell asleep together.

No idle chitchat. No false preening and silly flirting. Completely different from my usual. It felt more intimate than normal.

She left so quickly that I didn't get her number, but I didn't think that would be an issue. I figured I would see her on campus. Chesterboro isn't a huge school. It's hard to hide. But I never saw her again. I wondered if she had been visiting friends. It surprised me how disappointed I'd been over the missed opportunity.

What are the chances that this is her, after all this time? I grin, shaking my head. Slim. But suddenly, I'm not as turned off by the idea of participating. Besides, I'll get to rub it in Ellison's face when I beat him. And I will win this thing. I might not be excited to be doing it, but that doesn't mean I'm not going to dominate.

"All right. Hit me with all the details. I'm all in, Coach." I pull all the papers toward me.

Coach puts his hand on top, stopping me. "Make us look good out there, Mitch." He raises his brows in warning.

I try not to let it bother me that he's still unsure about me. Standing, I press a mock-outraged hand against my chest. "I always look good. And when am I ever anything but on my best behavior?"

He retracts his hand, and I gather the papers. He's still muttering to himself as I leave.

Ivy

I DON'T RECOGNIZE MANY people at the Dancing Across the Campus tryouts. I raise my chin and act like that doesn't bother me. I've been on stage since I was a child, so I know how to pretend. It's not their fault that they don't know me either. Most of them are probably sophomores. There are a couple of juniors I've seen before. They're here to do the same thing I am—build their portfolio. I'm just a year behind.

It should be my last semester at Chesterboro, a light one. Instead, I've got a loaded schedule, and I'll still have to finish a few classes in the summer to get my diploma. It's amazing I'm managing that, even. I've been off campus for two semesters. But my advisors let me take some core classes online, and I squeezed in a few studio classes in the city this fall that the advisors accepted for transfer credit.

That doesn't make up for the huge gap in my performance portfolio, though. At this rate, the best I can hope is that my portfolio will help me secure some tryouts for dance troupes in the area. I'm open to dancing anywhere in the Northeast, but I'm lacking the recent experience they'll be looking for. I guess that's what happens when Hodgkin's lymphoma puts your life on hold.

I shake that off. If I've learned anything this year, it's that there's nothing to gain from dwelling on things out of my control. That's over now. I can only move forward from here, and that means pushing through this fundraiser publicity stunt.

It was my advisor's idea. She said that it was a chance for me to get back on campus, to ease back into college life. She also suggested that I do my own choreography instead of letting one of the other students do it. She didn't have to say that it would help me prove that even after putting my body through hell, I still have what it takes.

If she needs proof, then that's what I'll give her, even if that means dancing with the captain of the debate team or the president of the student government. Not only am I a solid dancer, but I'm a good teacher and an even better choreographer. This is a golden opportunity for me.

I run through my stretches, warming up my muscles, grinning. There were times, in the first couple of months of treatment, when I didn't even want to stand up. It took me months to get my body back into condition. I'll never take its strength for granted again.

Around me, some of the others chat. The girl next to me is alone, so I smile at her. "Hi. I'm Ivy."

"Hey. Olivia." She stretches out her shoulders. "Are you new?"

It's an innocent question. I left midway through fall semester last year. Even if she's a junior now, there's no reason she would remember me. Still, it stings, the reminder of everything I've missed. That's why I'm here, though: to take my life back. I widen my grin. "No. I had to take some time off, that's all. I'm a senior. I'll be back in the spring."

"Cool." She smiles. "Welcome back, then. How did you get dragged into this?" She rolls her eyes. "I thought they only pawned this off on those new to the major."

"Champion suggested it. To beef up my portfolio." Madame Champion is my advisor. "Like I said, I took time off. I need some exposure."

I can tell she wants to ask more questions, but there's no polite way to do it, so she only nods, and I'm glad. I don't want to talk about it. I don't want to be the cancer girl on campus, singled out for pity or special attention. I'm determined to get my life back to normal. We continue warming up as the participants arrive. I don't recognize many of them. "Hey," I whisper to my new friend. "Give me the scoop. Do you know any of these people?"

She scoots closer to me, a glint of mischief in her eyes. I lean in. I can tell I'm going to like her. She nods her head toward a tall guy with short black hair. As he looks us over, I only think that he's got striking features and kind eyes. "That's Marcus Johnson. He's the captain of the basketball team."

I nod, taking in his frame. I should have guessed he was an athlete—he carries himself like he's comfortable in his own body. I make a note that I should pick the athletes with my votes. Natural ability will help me teach them the dances. Marcus Johnson is on my list.

Today, we're going to dance with each of the participants. Then they'll vote for their three top choices for partners, and we'll do the same. My advisor and two other dance instructors in the program will divide us into pairs. Then we'll need to learn three different dance routines to put on during two different shows in the spring. After the first show, though, some pairs will be eliminated. They haven't given us all the scoring criteria yet. The first step, though, is choosing partners.

Requirement one for me: athletic.

A couple of girls come in together, and Olivia marks them as the head cheerleader and the president of one of the sororities.

"Who's that?" I ask, motioning to a tall blond guy with too much swagger.

"That's Roman Ellison. He's the quarterback for the football team. I'm surprised the coach let him participate. They have championships coming up. But they just had a really big scandal a couple weeks ago, over Thanksgiving break. One of their tight ends, Teddy Little, was arrested for assault. Some sorority girl. Heard he messed her up pretty bad." She shakes her head, frowning. "I'm guessing Roman's presence is a peace offering to the campus."

I wrinkle my nose, and my stomach hurts for the girl I don't even know. But that wasn't this guy—it was his teammate. Roman looks athletic. He stays on my potential partner list.

I glance back at the door in time to see Declan Mitchell walk through. Everything in my body stills. If it's possible, he's even bigger and better-looking than he was a year ago. His hair is longer, falling across his face. There's nothing fancy about what he's wearing—gym shorts, a hoodie, and sneakers like the other guys. But he makes the outfit look better than they do. I can feel his confidence from across the room.

I duck my head, wondering if he'll recognize me. It's been over a year, and I can't imagine the snuggle session we had made any impression on him. I can't decide if I want him to remember me or not, and it bothers me it might be both.

"That's Declan Mitchell, the hockey team captain." Olivia leans closer as if the next part is really juicy. "Huge flirt and playboy. Don't know how serious he'll take something like this."

Even now, I close my eyes, embarrassed. I don't know what I'd been thinking that night before I left. I should be happy that all we did was cuddle. I couldn't find my way around a playboy like him if someone drew me a diagram and gave me a compass.

I'm ridiculous. He's not going to remember me. I barely recognize myself from that girl a year ago, and it's not only the shorter hair. That girl had been a soldier, preparing to go to war. Now, I'm home from that battle, and I'm not the same.

Olivia might be right. He's naturally athletic, sure. But I need someone who is going to take this seriously. Declan's reputation precedes him, and if what Olivia says is still true, I also doubt his devotion to winning this thing. There are going to be practices. It's going to require some time.

Declan seems risky.

My eyes are drawn to him. I don't want to watch him, though, and I definitely don't want to get caught watching him. So, I cast glances at him from the side, keeping my face averted, pretending to be consumed with my stretches. He joins Roman Ellison, and they do that handshake, back smack thing that guys do. He repeats the motion with Marcus Johnson. I'm too far away to hear what they say, but they all laugh, and the smile on his face hits me in the stomach.

Declan is almost obscenely good-looking.

As Madame Champion calls for our attention, I stand and stretch my neck. I only have a few opportunities to showcase my skills this semester, and now isn't the time to get distracted by some guy I've said a handful of words to, no matter how gorgeous he is. I need to focus on winning this competition.

"Welcome to the initial ratings for the Dancing Across the Campus competition." Madame Champion smiles at our group, about two or three dozen people. "We in the performing arts department here at Chesterboro are incredibly excited about this new fundraising endeavor. We will divide the money we raise from ticket sales into thirds. We'll use some of it to fund improvements here, to our beloved theater. We will funnel another third back to the winning participant's sport or activity. The last third will be donated to a local foundation devoted to bringing the performing arts to underprivileged children."

There is polite applause. Madame continues, "Today, we'll pair our contestants off with dancers from the program. In the middle, we'll take a break to mingle. At the end of our time, you'll be asked to rank your top three choices for partners." She motions toward the other two instructors from the program. "This evening, my colleagues and I will use your suggestions and our own assessments to create the pairings we feel will give you the best chances for success in the competition. We will email you those pairings tomorrow. The rest of the week, there will be studio time if you'd like to get together. We will resume practicing after the holiday."

She returns to a table and lifts a stack of numbers, holding them up. "Each of you will pin a number on your clothes. Make note of the partners you feel most complement you." She hands the numbers to the closest dancer, who takes one and passes the stack along. "Will my department's dancers please line up against the wall?"

I collect my number and a safety pin before following her instructions, taking my place against the mirrors with the others.

I feel someone looking at me, and when I glance up, I find Declan's eyes on me. I don't understand the look on his face, but I get the feeling he definitely remembers me.

Declan

IT'S HER—IVY, FROM A year ago.

Except she looks different than I remember. Her hair is short. Not a pixie cut, but it's only a few inches long. Still the same lovely brunette color and a mess of waves. The style looks great on her, accentuating her strong jawline and cupid-bow lips.

Her dance outfit is skintight, showing off those long legs. Those are definitely the same. But there's a tattoo now, too, on her collarbone. It's a dainty thing, and I can't make out what it is from here. She hadn't struck me as the tattoo sort when I met her last year, but it looks hot on her.

The lead instructor teaches us a basic waltz step. I don't know much about ballroom dancing, but this seems pretty straightforward. She puts the guys on one side of the room and the girls on the other, like a middle school dance. I go forward with the left foot, sideways with the right, then close with the left. Then I go back with the right side with the left, and close with the right. A box. They teach the ladies the reverse. Before long, they've got us paired off and start playing music.

It's something classical. I like it, even though I'm not familiar with it, but I like most music.

My first partner is really short, and I get the impression that my size overwhelms her. She misses her cue, stepping on my feet. I smooth things over. By the time we switch partners, she's laughing. My next partner is taller, but she's got a flirtatious look on her face. Her name is Dina or Dana or something. I miss it. She makes a comment about the size of my biceps. I don't usually have an issue with that, but I feel like I've seen her at Shepherd before, and she might hook up with a sophomore on the team. I'm not about to mess around with that.

I breathe a sigh of relief when we switch.

The next girl is the one I saw Ivy talking to earlier. Time to get some information.

"Hey," I start with a smile. "I'm Declan Mitchell."

She allows me to step us through the waltz, even as she pins me with an assessing stare. "I know who you are." She cocks her head, gracefully following my lead. "I'm Olivia."

"Hi. So, tell me... how do you know Ivy Deveraux?"

Her eyebrows shoot up. "Ivy?" Her eyes drift to where Ivy's stumbling along with the head of the debate team. "I just met her tonight. I've never seen her before. She said she took some time off from school."

Interesting. "She did? Why?"

She scowls at me. "I didn't ask. I told you—I just met her."

"Right." I grin at her.

"You're actually pretty graceful." She sounds surprised.

"Thanks?" *What does that mean?* The bell rings, ending our time. "See you later, Olivia."

It's two more dances before I'm paired with Ivy. I smile when our names are called, finding her gaze in the room. Her expression isn't as enthused. In fact, she winces.

My grin fades. *What's that all about?*

As we meet on the dance floor, I salute her. "Hey, Ivy. Long time, no see." I can see now that the tattoo along her collar is a branch with oak leaves and acorns. It's skilled artistry.

"Declan." She raises her arms so we can step into a dancing position. The music starts, and I slide us into the steps. This waltzing stuff is easy. "I didn't think you'd remember me."

I ignore that. "How have you been?"

"I'm good now." She isn't making eye contact, only staring over my shoulder. But like that night last year, we move together as if our bodies know exactly what the other will do, completely in sync. "How are you?"

"I'm good." This is stupid small talk. I don't know if I'm having a hard time because she feels so fucking good against me or something else, but I'm generally more interesting than this. "Listen, I tried to find you last year…"

"Why?" she interrupts me. She's wide-eyed, like she's confused.

"Why?" I repeat. "Because I wanted to see you." I curl my fingers around her waist, shifting my grip. The curve of her hip in my palm has my mind going to places where hand-over-clothes contact rarely sends it.

"Again, why?" She meets my eyes. I only have a moment to realize that they're a cool-gray color before her gaze slides away again. "Some girl you didn't even hook up with? Why bother?"

I can only blink at her.

She cringes. "Sorry. That's nice of you, I guess." She glances down at my feet, studying my form. We're dancing circles around the rest of these stiffs. "So… are you planning to take this competition seriously?"

"As a heart attack," I shoot back. "How about you?"

She narrows her eyes at me. "I'm not joking, Declan. Are you going to really do your best in this thing?"

"I just said I would. Why?"

"You kind of have a reputation."

"Do I?"

She scowls at me. "You know you do."

"What's my reputation, Princess?" This should be good.

Her face flushes the prettiest pink. "You know…"

I shake my head, playing dumb.

"You're a flirt. A playboy."

There are worse things she could have called me. "What does being a flirt or a playboy have to do with the competition?"

"I want someone who is going to take this seriously."

"I just told you I want to win." I furrow my brows at her. "I'm competitive. I play hockey."

"Right." She still looks skeptical.

I catch the head instructor staring at us, and I give her a head bob and a wink.

In return, she clicks her tongue at us. "Very nice, Ms. Deveraux."

A scowl settles on Ivy's forehead as the music stops, and the boss lady moves on. She steps out of my grasp immediately, and my arms feel empty without her. She crosses her arms over her chest, shaking her head. "No. I don't think so."

"What?" *Did I miss something?*

"No offense, Declan, but I don't think I want you as my partner." She spins, heading toward the table with the drinks.

"Wait." I grab her wrist to stop her. "What do you mean?"

"I mean, don't put me down on your voting paper." She enunciates sharply, as if I'm an idiot or can't understand English.

I cross my arms over my chest. "Why not? What's the matter with you?"

"Not me. You."

"I'm sorry?" I'm sure I'm not following correctly. This is physically the same girl from a year ago, but she's not the same. That girl was into me. There was a spark, I was sure of it. This one is closed off, not just physically different. "Me?"

"You..." She inhales, smoothing a hand over her short curls. "Because... you." She waves her hand over me. "With your too-charming smile and your winks and your playboy reputation." She rolls her eyes. "And your 'I tried to find you.'" The way she mimics me is impressive. "Just... I don't have the emotional bandwidth for this."

"Whoa, there." I hold up my hands. She's way overthinking this. "This is a dance competition, not a marriage proposal. I'm only looking for the person who can help me win because I plan to be the best."

"Don't flatter yourself."

"Oh, it's not flattery, Princess, it's the truth." I grin at her. "I'm going to be part of the winning team. I'll bring you along if you'd like."

"No," she shoots over her shoulder at me as she snags a bottle of water off the table.

"No?" *Seriously*? She must see that we'd be the best fit. She's smart. I can tell.

She shakes her head. "No, thank you. I think you'll be a distraction that I don't need. I want someone who's going to focus."

"Is everything all right here?" One of the other instructors, a tall, thin guy, stares at us from across the table.

Ivy smiles at him, all sweetness. "We're wonderful, Mr. Lefleur. No problems at all." She turns that smile on me. "I'm serious, Declan. Don't." She nods at me, then spins away, leaving me there.

"Ivy," I offer and chuckle as I watch her go. In her tight dance outfit, the curves of her are all on display. She's thin and all muscle, but the ratio of her waist and hips is art, and those legs... I shift to adjust myself in my shorts and reach for a bottle of water.

Miss Ivy might think that I'm not a good option for her partner, but as far as I can tell, she's the best dancer here... at least for me. We fit. I wasn't lying—if it gives me an edge in this contest, I'll request her to work with me. Coach wants me to make the team look good, and that's what I plan to do. Besides, it's not in me to approach a contest with anything less than my full attention.

That has nothing to do with the attraction I feel for her. As far as I'm concerned, that's just a bonus.

The bell rings to switch partners again, and I step up to my new one. But through the last three partners, my eyes continue to find Ivy.

Ivy

I BREEZE INTO MADAME Champion's office the day after tryouts, my phone clasped in a white-knuckle grip, the email listing Declan as my partner on the screen. "Madame, I respectfully disagree with this pairing. Declan Mitchell and I are not a good fit."

"Hello, Ms. Deveraux." Madame sits back from her computer, a half-smile on her face. "How are you today?"

Right. That was rude, and Madame is a stickler about manners. "Good afternoon, Madame. I hope you're well."

"I am, dear. And you? Feeling well?"

I nod. "Yes, ma'am. Better than ever." Sometime soon, I hope everyone stops asking me how I'm feeling as often as they do now. She's only being thoughtful, but I hate feeling like I'm worrying everyone all the time.

She taps a pen against her desk. "Now, what can I do for you?"

I inhale. "Madame... I ask you to reconsider my pairing for the competition."

"Yes, you said you and Mr. Mitchell aren't a good fit." She steeples her fingers and pins me with an assessing stare. "May I ask why?"

I open my mouth, then close it. All the immediate reasons are on the tip of my tongue. He's too good-looking, and his smile makes my stomach feel like jelly. But that's not going to dissuade Madame. "He's a huge playboy and takes nothing seriously."

I quash a flare of guilt. That's not fair. I don't know him well enough to make that assessment for sure. I'm going off his reputation and my gut reactions to him. If anything, he was more confident and determined to win than I was. I don't really have to win—I only need to put on a good show and choreograph my butt off.

Madame leans forward and sifts through the contents of her desk. She snatches up a piece of paper. "This says that he's very serious about having you as his partner." She pushes the slip of paper across to me. It's one of the voting sheets, his name on the top in tidy block letters. In the same efficient print, he'd written my name in all three of the slots.

I grit my teeth. Of course, after I told him not to choose me, he would do something like that. I feel that Declan Mitchell doesn't like being told what to do. I exhale, shaking my head. "Madame…"

"It's obvious you made an impression on him." I'm not certain, but it looks like she's suppressing a grin.

"I told him I didn't want to dance with him."

Her brow furrows. "Miss Deveraux, that's not how we compose ourselves in this department," she scolds. "This is part fundraiser, but also a campus outreach exercise. You are an emissary for the Performing Arts department."

I rub my forehead. "I know!" I soften my tone. "But… he bothers me."

"Why?" She tilts her head.

That's the million-dollar question. I search for the right words. "He's arrogant and… and he's a playboy." He's also stupidly good-looking, and his smile makes me feel melty.

"You said that. But this is a dance competition, not a dating competition."

"I know." Good thing, too. I couldn't win a dating competition. I cross my arms over my chest. This isn't going the way I'd hoped.

Madame leans back in her chair, studying me as she taps her lips with her finger. Finally, she raises her chin. "I don't agree with your assessment, and I'm not willing to shuffle the partners around. If you have no pressing reason to reject Mr. Mitchell, and you have presented none, then we will leave the pairings as they are."

"Madame—"

She raises her hand to stop me. "Mr. Mitchell appears to have a lot of natural skills. There are a few of participants who I believe might be difficult to work with, who do not possess the grace or natural ability that would be preferable for a brief introduction to dance as this is. But I suspect he will do well in this competition. And you need an adequate partner if any of your performances are to be used as portfolio showcase pieces." She taps her fingers against her desk, and her next words are softer. "Truthfully, Miss Deveraux, I believe you're seeing this all wrong. All three of us on the judging panel agree that when you danced with Mr. Mitchell, there was… *attirance…*" She shakes her head, realizing she needs to translate for me. "A pull. Something magnetic. We believe that you two will make an electric pairing."

That sounds unpredictable and dangerous, and I've already spent a year dealing with unpredictable and dangerous things.

Right now, I want solid and safe. I want to take back control of my life. There's nothing controllable about Declan Mitchell. He's bottled lightning, and I have no desire to get burned. "I don't think…"

She holds up her hand. "Find some time to meet with him in the studio this week. I have all the faith that you will connect with him. I fully expect that you and Mr. Mitchell will be one of the most watchable couples in our competition. When we return from holiday, if you feel the same, we'll revisit this issue."

By then, we'll be closing in on the first competition date. It'll be too late to switch. But I can tell that the case is closed for Madame. For all her composure and sophistication, she's stubborn. If she's made this decision, there's nothing I can do about it. "Of course. Thank you, Madame. Have a good day." I stand, retrieve my bag from the floor, and throw it over my shoulder.

At the door, she stops me. "Miss Deveraux?" When I glance back at her, she smiles. "Try to have some fun with this."

Declan Mitchell sets off fireworks inside my body. When I don't find him impossibly attractive, his flirting and teasing unsettle me. I have no idea how working with him is going to be fun. At best, I hope I don't strangle him. I force a sickly smile. "Right. Fun."

I'm not sure, but I think I hear her chuckle as I breeze out her office door.

Declan

I'M LATE FOR REHEARSAL with Ivy. I got a text from her yesterday. I assume it was Ivy, anyway. It didn't give much information. All it said was, *our first rehearsal is on Wednesday at seven o'clock. Be there on time or else.* Just the facts, a bit of a threat.

Definitely Ivy.

I almost asked if she could clarify what "or else" entailed and if it was kinky, but I doubted she'd appreciate my humor. Instead, I sent a thumbs up. I planned to be there on time, but practice ran over, and I needed to have a conversation with the second line. One winger is a sophomore, but though he's young, he shows a lot of talent. He's playing too low in the defensive zone, then not breaking out fast enough when the defenders pass the puck up. I ended up having to sit with him to explain because Coach was working with the goalie.

I take the stairs two at a time, skipping around a couple of other people. I round the corner to the studio we're assigned to and find Ivy standing near the back of the room with her arms crossed. Even with the pissed-off look on her face, she's gorgeous. Her short, dark hair is in a riotous mass of curls. She's wearing some sort of tights and an athletic top shows off the oak branch tattoo along her collarbone. When I join her, she scowls at me. "You're late."

"By five minutes." I blow out an exhale. "I needed to stay late at the rink. One of my wingers needed some insight into our offensive system."

She wrinkles her nose. "You have a system to offend people?"

The comment surprises me, and my laugh comes out in a bark. "No." I grin. "He's a forward, and there are different systems out there for how to play the position. Our coach prefers our wingers to get low in the defensive zone but then move to the boards to wait for a defender pass to break out." I shrug. "He wasn't doing it right. I was helping him."

She crosses her arms over her chest. "I need your help here." She gestures to the empty studio. "After this weekend, the building will be closed for two weeks for the holiday. If you want to win like you said you did, you'll need to work hard. You're naturally athletic, but you don't know these dances. I need you to take this seriously."

"We've danced before." I grin at her, mirroring her crossed-arm stance. "We have natural chemistry. I'm sure we'll get it."

She huffs and drops her gaze. She shifts her weight, dropping one of her arms so she's cupping her elbow. "I think we need to clear the air about something." She straightens, pinning me with a hard stare. "That night, last year… you said you were going through some things, and I was too. It was a strange night for me, and I don't know what you think happened or what perceived connection you think we had." She squares her shoulders. "I can assure you, though, that nothing is going to happen between us. I need to impress my advisor during this competition. We don't have time to mess around. We're here to dance. That's it."

I study her. This girl is much different from the girl I met a year ago. She's more serious, maybe... though that's not quite it either. She was intense that night as well. But she's sharper, more wary, and definitely closed off.

It was clear by the end of ratings that I hadn't misjudged Ivy's talent—I didn't dance with anyone who compared to her. Not only do we naturally connect, but she's got presence on the dance floor. I get the impression that dancing is like hockey that way—it's not only about raw talent but also character and charisma, the personal magic that a person brings to the floor. If I want to win, I need to have her as a partner. I put her down in all the voting slots, even though I knew she said she didn't want me.

But if I'm reading this right, she just wants someone who's going to kick ass in this thing. I'm that guy. She just doesn't know it yet.

"I'm sorry I was late today, but I promise, I'm very serious about winning this competition. I'm the captain of my team this year. My coach wants me to put a good face on our organization, and that's what I'm going to do." I make a cross over my heart. "From here on, I'm completely on board."

She still looks skeptical. "You'll be here on time. And you'll follow my directions?"

"Absolutely."

"And no funny business."

"I have no idea what you mean."

"You know..." she scowls at me. "No flirting and being charming and whatever else it is that you do."

"Flirty and charming is who I am, Princess."

I might be wrong, but I swear she growls at me. "I mean, there can't be anything personal or... physical between us."

I grin at her, then raise my palms, all innocence. "Fine. I read you loud and clear. We're partners on the dance floor and nowhere else. I promise that I'll be all work and no play here." I wink at her, and she rolls her eyes. "Unless you change your mind."

"I won't."

"So you say." I shrug. "You're missing an opportunity, though. I'm great in bed."

Her face flushes as she drops her head, and it surprises me how hot I find the reaction. When she breathes out a shaky laugh, my dick goes hard. I shrug nonchalantly but turn from her and use the chance to regroup.

Warning bells go off in my head. Her entire response screams innocence, and that shit rarely does it for me. Innocence means inexperience, and I don't do that. Despite my playboy reputation, I stick to girls who know what to expect, who are ready for a good time, and who will walk away at the end as satisfied as I do. Girls who will sign up for short-term and who won't get hurt.

I clench my jaw. I need to keep a hard lock on whatever physical attraction we have going on here. I've been around the block, and I'm no schoolboy. I can keep my body in check. I have to prove I can be a leader on my team, that I can put on a good face for my organization. Physical hijinks are not in the cards. Ivy's right—that stuff will be distracting. Sure, I'm attracted to her, but I also want to win, so I'm not taking any chances with my partner. We need to stay in our own lanes, so we'll do as she said—no funny business, just dance partners.

I file all of it away. To her, I grin and motion to the studio. "Tell me, boss. What are we doing today?"

She blinks at me before she recovers. "Um, right." She bends over, giving me an amazing view of her perfect ass, and retrieves an iPad from a beat-up leather bag. She flicks her fingers across the screen before handing it to me. "I'm going to be choreographing the dances we'll do in the competition. There will be two dances on the first night of competition, and then if we make it to the final round, we'll dance on the second night as well."

"We'll make it to the second round." Between her talent and my natural ability and work ethic, we've got this.

She continues as if I didn't speak. "This is my part of the first routine that we'll be doing. It's open style, a combination of hip-hop, jazz, krump, and popping."

I recognize hip-hop and jazz, but not the rest. Glancing at the screen, I watch her move. The volume's too low for me to hear what song she chose, but even without the music, she's captivating. Her movements are powerful, intentional, and graceful. When her part is over, she starts another video. "This will be your part."

I'm impressed when it's over. As the video stops, I glance up at her. "I've got to admit… I'm good, but I can't do this yet. Are you sure you can teach me?"

She flashes a cocky grin on her cupid lips. "I can teach anyone."

I recognize the confidence in her. It's how I feel on the ice rink. I don't doubt she can do what she says she can, but something about her makes me want to tease her, to get a rise out of her. To see the cracks in her armor. She's just so damn somber. So I look her over, pretending to be skeptical. "I don't know, Princess..."

She props her hands on her hips, competition in her face. "Are you scared, Mitchell? Because you sound scared."

My smile widens. *Game on.* "Never. I was born ready." I rewind the video. "Let's do this."

The next hour is a blur of her teaching me my part of the dance. She's used the song "Can I Have This Dance" by Francis and the Lights. As I see how her part will play against mine in the performance, my respect for her talent increases. The way she's structured the steps, the dance tells a story. Her role is as the experienced one, teaching my character in the dance how to move. In the beginning, my part acts uncertain about the steps, and her part is confident and elaborate as she teaches me the dance. In the last bridge, there's a connection between the two parts, and they sync up. She's even mapped out a place where we might add a flip or a turn.

It's smart, juxtaposing the two of us this way, a sly nod to my reputation. From what I can tell, this show will essentially be a popularity contest, with the audience voting on their favorite performers. People have accused me of a lot of things —being a player, being arrogant, being selfish. But this dance pokes fun at that just enough.

At the end of our time, she forwards me the two videos she made—one of her parts, one of mine. Then she sends a video of us performing together. I can't tell if she's pleased with our progress or not.

Back at my place, I play the videos on repeat. Except the more I watch them, the more I feel that something is off between the three videos. When she's performing our parts separately, the routines are amazing. But when I watch us together…

I'm squinting at the screen when my roommate, Griffin Parker, knocks on my open door. "Hey, Mitch. Can I borrow some tape? I'll get some more when I'm out tomorrow."

I reach into my drawer and grab a roll of white hockey tape. Barely looking at him, I throw it across the room, and he catches it easily in one hand. I tilt my head at the screen. I split the screen to watch the videos simultaneously next to each other.

"What's that?" Griff stands next to me as he rips the used hockey tape from the toe of his hockey stick. "Scratch that. Who is that?"

The interest in his voice makes me scowl up at him. "Prohibited." Even considering Ivy with Griff makes my jaw clench.

He opens his hands. "Gotcha." He leans closer. "Is this the dance competition thing?"

"Yeah, this is my partner, Ivy."

"I've never seen her before." Griff cocks his head, his eyebrows raised.

I get it. Ivy is gorgeous. No way she'd be on campus without any of my guys noticing her.

"She's really… talented."

I narrow my eyes at him, and he only smiles. "Yeah."

"Why do you look pissed, then? If I got to spend a bunch of time with that pretty thing, I wouldn't have that sourpuss look on my face."

"Something about this routine doesn't jibe with me." I can't quite put my finger on it.

He leans in. Together, we watch the videos again. "She looks so… grim," he finally says.

She does. There's businesslike and professional, but the look on her face is severe. For a dance about a girl trying to coax a guy into dancing with her, she looks somber enough to be attending a funeral.

I stop the videos. "Interesting." I hold my hand out to my friend, and he smacks it. "Thanks."

He clearly has no idea what I'm talking about, but he nods and holds up the tape. "Thanks for this. I'll replace it."

"No problem."

As I watch him go, I run through my steps. I've got another hour. When we get together tomorrow, I'm going to be ready.

Ivy

THANKS TO DECLAN'S PRACTICE schedule, I could only book a half an hour in the studio the next day. I'm not sure that it's even worth it, but he shows up five minutes early. That's a good sign.

He swore he was going to take this seriously, but I wasn't sure I believed him. But even though it doesn't seem like Declan can talk without flirting, he surprised me yesterday with his determination to pick up the steps. He stayed on task the entire time. Not only that, but he picked them up easier than I could have even hoped.

Now, he's here early. If I can learn to ignore all his teasing, maybe this won't be the disaster I was sure it would be.

In loose sweatpants, a T-shirt, and wet hair, he's so good-looking that it's almost hard to look at him. I sigh. This would be a lot easier if he wasn't so attractive. I drop my bag next to the stereo. "Did you just come from practice?" I ask.

"Yeah. I showered, though. Trust me, that's not a smell you need to be familiar with." He drops his gym bag on the floor next to mine. "I wanted to show you something. Did you bring your tablet?"

I can smell the shampoo on him, and soap never smelled so good. I'm immediately wary. "Of course."

"Okay. Good. Can you videotape us?"

"You want to dance right now?" I figured we would need to go over the steps again, that I would spend the short time we had answering questions. I didn't expect him to want to attempt the full piece.

"Unless you aren't ready." He waggles his eyebrows at me. "I mean, I guessed I would have to carry you in this thing, but…"

I can't help it—I laugh. "You wish. I could dance rings around you with my hands tied behind my back."

His lips fall into a lazy grin, and he raises his palms. "I didn't ask about your kink preferences." He winks at me.

He's messing around. Declan says stuff for shock value. I get that. So why does my face heat? I grit my teeth and reach for my bag, happy to have something to distract me. Pulling out my tablet, I cue up the music and connect my Bluetooth to the studio's speakers. It takes another moment to prop the iPad up on a chair and point the camera where we'll be working. If he says he's ready to go, let's see what he's got.

I take my first position, and Declan arranges himself next to me. As the first beats of the song play, I start into my part of the routine, and he matches my movements. For the first four beats, I'm surprised, but then I fall into the flow of the dance.

Except, when I choreographed this piece, I didn't fully appreciate what it would be like to dance it with Declan. I mean, I had the idea of the routine last week when Madame approached me about the competition. When I tweaked the moves on Monday and yesterday, I knew it was with Declan in mind, so that's not it either. No, I didn't expect to his nearness to affect me this much. I didn't plan for the force of his personality, the heat that I would feel touching his hands, brushing against him, and making repeated eye contact with his intense gaze.

I'm a performer, though, and I hold it together.

When the last strains end, I'm in his arms. I purposely ended the dance with me in a dip. I like the story the routine tells. The movements start with me, the experienced dancer, teaching him the steps, to him mastering the steps and meeting me in the end as an equal. The song I chose is upbeat, and it puts a smile on my face. I want us to go out there in our first showing and make people grin. After all, audiences want to be entertained.

But being held in his arms, with his forearms pressed into my back, cradling the base of my head in his hands... it's an intimate position, with my weight on him. I assumed he could manage it, what with all that muscle coating him. He practically oozes strength and confidence, and I counted on it when I choreographed. I didn't count on me, though, because lying in his arms, completely relying on him to hold me, is disconcerting... and exciting.

My breathing is heavy because we just danced our asses off, but my heart races. His gaze is intense, like a caress, and I'm off balance. I must be because I'm dying for his touch, on my face, my neck, wherever his eyes trail.

I shift my feet back and return the weight to my own legs, grasping for my composure. Relying on him to hold me up is shorting some vital systems in my brain.

I stumble as I struggle to stand, reaching for something to say to regain control of myself, of this situation. "You learned all the moves."

"You sent me the videos," he responds, his brows creased. "You said you wanted me to learn the dance."

He's not wrong. "Yes, but I didn't expect you to,"—I wave my hand at the dance floor—"I didn't expect you to be that good yet." As soon as the words are out, I brace myself for his response.

He doesn't disappoint. "You have no idea how good I am, Princess."

"Stop calling me that," I snap. "I thought you said you were going to knock it off. Can you even talk without flirting?"

He cocks his head, his mouth twisting as if he's really thinking about the question. "I mean, probably. But why? Flirting is so much fun." He waves a hand. "Anyway, that wasn't really flirting. I just say stuff. Mostly to make fun of myself. Because it's ironic."

I don't know what he's talking about, so I shake my head.

He shrugs. "But I'm only messing around. I fully intend to stand by what I said. Nothing physical between us. We agreed." He buries his hands in his pockets.

I breathe out an exasperated huff and throw my hands up, using the opportunity to turn away from him. He's not wrong, though. That is what I said.

I return to where I've propped up the tablet, happy to put some space between us. Snatching it up, I navigate to the video as I suck in a few steadying breaths. When I'm sure I've got myself together, I return to his side and cue us up.

As we watch together, I'm so hyperaware of the heat of him next to me I can barely focus on the video. Luckily for me, he suggests we watch it a second time. "This time, watch our faces," he says.

I do as he instructs, wondering what he's getting at. I can't help but notice how effortlessly he's learned the steps. If he's going to pick up all our dances this fast, I can definitely include more complicated movements. That opportunity fills me with excitement.

"Do you see that?" He points his finger at the iPad. "I watched this over and over last night, and I couldn't get over how the two pieces weren't connecting." He takes a few steps away from me. With little effort, he dives into the middle of my routine and performs a handful of moves with no music or prompting. He stops, completely unaware of how difficult learning not one but two routines in a day is, and joins me again, his face animated. "The dance is amazing. You are obviously talented as a choreographer." The compliment warms me, but he keeps talking as if what he said was obvious. "But the story... I feel like we're not telling this story the way we should."

Still buzzing from the compliment, I ask, "What do you mean?"

"You're all... laced up." He waves over me. "Everything about you is controlled, assured... totally solemn, right until the end." He motions for the iPad, and I hand it over mutely. He swipes his finger to skim through the video. "Look at your face here." He lets it play for a few moments before skipping forward. "Then here." He lets it roll longer this time. "Now watch me."

He starts the video from the beginning, and this time he hands it to me. I lift it so I can see us closer. Halfway through, it's clear what he's talking about.

I look like a robot. Not in my movements. Mechanically, my dancing is on target, right down to the curve of my hands and the points of my toes. But my expressions... I look stoic, grave. There's no real animation in me at all.

He continues, "This story is about you teaching me. But you've devised it so that by the end, we're in the same place. Drawn together, equals, happy. So, if it's going to be great, your part needs to go from being all tightly wound to being..."

"Vulnerable," I whisper, still staring at the screen.

"What?"

I hitch my chin up and meet his eyes. "You're right." I point at the tablet. "This dance is about someone asking the other for trust, and my expressions need to show that."

"Ivy... you're making this too complicated." He exhales an exasperated puff. "This is supposed to be fun. It's a fun song, a fun dance." He points to the iPad. "You don't look like you're having fun."

That's his holdup? I blink at him. "You think I'm not having fun?"

"That's what's missing here." He digs a hand through his shaggy hair. "We're dancing. Moving our bodies around. It's fun." He pulls through the strands, leaving them disheveled. It's hot on him. "You're supposed to be having fun."

"I..." I search for words. "I see." It's not a suitable response, but though my performance in the video might not show vulnerability, I feel split open, like he's able to see into the heart of me.

"People have looked like they've had more fun at root canals, Princess. You're aloof. Actually, I don't know what you are. But you don't look relaxed or like you're having a good time. That much, I'm sure of."

I'm sure Madame Champion mentioned fun when I spoke to her, but I shook her suggestion off. I stretch my memory, searching for when I truly had fun doing anything. The past year has been hellish—frightening, exhausting, and infuriating. There hasn't been time for fun. Even before that, I danced because I wanted a life full of working with other dancers and artists. That dream used to fill me with single-minded determination, and everything moved me toward it. When I felt better, I wanted—no, needed—to get my life back on that path. I've been clawing my way to normalcy since then.

But am I having any fun?

I don't know. He's right about one thing, though—while we danced today, I couldn't relax. There's no way I would let down my guard in his arms.

Because I'm attracted to him. He might not recognize it, but that's the real problem. I'm the one who harped on him about keeping things serious, no physical stuff. My body has clearly not gotten the memo.

I fall into silence. He wrinkles his nose in question, but whatever he finds in my expression must make him think twice about asking. I'm glad. I drop my gaze to the iPad because I can't hold his eye contact. "You're right." I clutch the tablet against my chest. "You're exactly right."

"Thanks?" He tilts his head, scowling at me. "Why do you sound like I told you that your dog died?"

"I don't have a dog," I comment idly. "No, it's a good thing to know."

"Okay…" He's got that look, the what-the-hell-is-going-on face.

I can't reply, so I glance at the clock. Thankfully, our half hour is over. I force a smile. "We need to turn over the studio."

He scowls, pulling his phone out of his pocket to check the time. "Right."

"Can you practice tomorrow?" Even though a big part of me wants to run and hide from Declan Mitchell, I refuse. I've been through too much not to recognize what I'm feeling—it's fear, sharp and sickly. But I've done things scared before, and I'll do it again. I want my life back, the life I've always imagined, and this competition is my chance to put my skills on exhibition. As much as I hate to admit it, Declan was right about our partnership. We make a beautiful pairing. I'll just need to figure out how to do that without carving my heart out.

And without breaking my own rules. Even though I'm more attracted to Declan than I have been to any other guy in recent memory, getting involved with him physically is stupid on multiple levels. We have a competition to win, first. Plus, right now, I'm bruised inside and absolutely certain that Declan Mitchell can destroy me.

It's not his fault that I feel like the broken pieces of me are held together with tape. It's also on me that I'm so attracted to him. If I wasn't already such a mess, maybe he wouldn't be affecting me this way. Even as I consider that, I'm sure it's a lie. From the moment I laid eyes on him at that party last year, Declan's gotten under my skin.

This isn't running away. It's retreating and regrouping.

"I have hockey practice in the morning, from nine until lunch. After lunch is fine." It's obvious he doesn't like how this is ending, but I need to get away from him and his unspoken questions and be alone.

"Great. I'll set it up." I hurry to my bag, drop my tablet inside, and sling it over my shoulder. "I'll text you." With a wave, I leave without another word, hurrying out the door. I don't stop until I'm down the stairs and outside. Behind the building, I finally pause and let my bag drop to the pavement. I force myself to take deep breaths and process.

A strangled laugh squeaks out of me. I created a performance about trust when I'm not even sure I trust my own body. I certainly don't trust whatever powers are out there in the universe, pulling the strings. And I do not trust how drawn to Declan Mitchell I feel. He's a grenade thrown into the already volatile landscape of my life. Being around him is electric and dangerous, a roiling storm I can't control.

Righting myself, I square my shoulders and retrieve my bag. I head across the back parking lot and out onto the street. Action and doing... that's the only way to get through scary things. I need to go back to my room and watch the videos a million times until they're imprinted on me. That's obviously what Declan did.

I was wrong about him. Not only does he want to win—he's all in on this competition, and he's on target with the dance. Watching the video, it's clear he's devoted to the part he plays. I refuse to be anything less.

Tonight, I need to figure out a way to be vulnerable in our dances without letting down all my defenses with him. I just don't know how.

Declan

HOCKEY PRACTICE IS ROUGH the next morning as if Coach wants to work us over before we go on break for two weeks, game tomorrow be damned. It's probably fair. I plan to eat more sugar than the surgeon general would recommend and polish it off with eggnog and extra rum. I'm sure the rest of the guys feel the same. The season so far has been a mixed bag. We've had some huge wins, but our losses have been spectacular as well. We all need to recharge.

I check my phone after I get off the ice to find a text from Ivy, who set us up to practice tonight at seven. I reply with a quick note to say that's fine. I plan to head back to my place and snag a nap in between.

As I shrug my bag over my shoulder and head toward the parking lot, I replay last night's session again in my head. I've been doing that since she left the studio yesterday, but I still can't figure out what caused her to run away like her shoes were on fire. I tried to tell her, in as diplomatic a way as I could find, that she needed to relax. No one is going to believe that we're having a good time if she dances like she doesn't want to be there.

I just wanted her to loosen up. Then she started spouting stuff about trust and vulnerability, and I didn't know where to go with that. Truthfully, words like that scare the shit out of me. I wasn't looking for a commitment, for Christ's sake. I've never done commitment. I'm a strictly casual kind of guy. She made it crystal clear that she wants nothing to happen between us, and I agree with her. I get the impression that if she could calm down, we could have some fun. Honestly, I feel like we could even be friends.

Even as I consider friendship, though, the prospect of seeing her again sends a flash of lust through me. I squelch it hard. I already decided that would be a bad idea, but there's something about her that intrigues me. Sure, she's smart and pretty, but she's also driven. There's no way she could be such a talented dancer and so good at choreography if she wasn't devoted to her work. I admire shit like that.

We can be friends. I can do that. I might be a player, but I have other friends who are girls, like Shea Carmichael and Violet Tannehill, for example. They're great girls. Ivy's been off campus for a while. I don't know if she knows Shea and Vi. Maybe I could introduce her to them. I smile. The three of them will get along.

My phone buzzes in my pocket, and I drag it out, finding my stepmother's name on the screen. Well, the most recent stepmother. My father's been married four times, so I have two other ex-stepmothers as well. But Pam is the one he's still married to, at least for a little while longer. She filed for divorce right before Thanksgiving.

I swipe to answer, putting the phone to my ear. "Hey, Pam. How's it going?"

"Hi, Declan, hon. How are you?" She sounds frazzled.

"I'm good. What's up?" Pam doesn't call just to say hello.

"I was wondering… is there any chance that you and Stephen could get together, just the two of you, and do something fun while you're home over the holidays?"

"Sure." My youngest half-sibling, Pam's son, Stephen, is only seven, but he's a cool kid. "What do you think he'd like to do?"

"Oh, anything, I'm sure. As long as it's not at home and not with me or your father." She clips the last part, and I get an idea of what's really up.

"He's having a hard time with the divorce?" I offer, bracing myself. It's not that I don't like Pam—I just don't know her that well. After my parents split, I lived with my mom, and I only really see my father on holidays. He was married once between my mother and Pam, and I have two older sisters from his first marriage. They're both married, though. I also have a sister, Hillary, between Stephen and me. She's ten and in boarding school. She's a musical prodigy or something and plays the piano like a rockstar.

My half-siblings get together when we can—a few times a year—but it's hard because my father doesn't make much of an effort. He never does much in the way of parenting, so that's not surprising.

But I remember being seven. By then, my parents were already separated. Still, it was a confusing time. "Sure, Pam. Do you think he'd like to go skating with me?"

"That sounds great, Declan. Maybe you can talk to him."

That sounds ominous, but it can't be that hard to entertain a seven-year-old. "Absolutely. I'll text you when I get to my mom's this weekend." Though my father has a full floor in midtown Manhattan, my mother is in Brooklyn. "I'll let you know when I'll be in the city."

"Thanks." Her relief drifts over the line. "It means a lot to me."

We disconnect, and I stand next to my car, staring at the phone. Poor Stephen. What the hell am I going to say to him? "Sorry our dad is shit at marriage?" I feel bad for the kid. Luckily, he's got his mother, same as I do.

One thing I can say for my father is that he picks phenomenal wives. All four of the women he married are smart, beautiful, and caring. They're devoted mothers who fell in love with a charismatic rockstar who promised them the world and swore he could change. It's a shame they let my father break their hearts. I've watched it twice now. When he proposes, he's adamant that he's turned over a new leaf. Each time, he proves himself unreliable, unable to stick through things that are hard. It's not him that suffers. It's the women who expected him to be better that I feel sorry for.

It's the main reason I don't mess around with girls' emotions. I keep my relationships casual. I have no intention of breaking anyone's heart.

Declan

I HOPED THAT AFTER I chatted with Ivy that things would be better, and she could relax. But when we've almost finished the dance for the fifth time, I stop right in the middle of the floor. "Hold up."

Ivy pauses, stepping back, her hands on her hips. She's glistening, and I'm not sure I've ever seen a girl look this pretty covered in sweat. I force myself to ignore that. *Friends. We can only be friends.*

Today, as we've practiced, she's become twitchier and more irritable. This still isn't the vibe we want to give off. If anything, it's worse than yesterday.

"Let's take a break." I head to my bag, grab the water bottle I brought with me, and suck down a sip. I search my brain for a way to fix this.

Ivy growls in frustration. "We don't need a break. We need to get this."

"Princess, we have the dance. That's not our problem." I smile, but it's tight. I'm trying to hold my patience, but that's never been my strong suit. I toss the water bottle back into my bag.

"What's our problem, then?" She throws up her hands, clearly as frustrated as I am.

Obviously, we can't dance around this, pun intended. If we can't avoid the problem, we need to face it head-on. "You're cringing away from me." I sigh. "When you tense up every time I touch you, we're bound to look like puppets." I prop my hands on my hips. "Like I said yesterday, this will be a lot easier if you relax. Just have fun."

"Seriously. I'm trying." She exhales an exasperated huff. "But you make me nervous." Her eyes scan the studio, looking anywhere but at me. "You make me nervous, and I don't know how to fix that."

Everything inside me stills. That is not what I expected her to say. "Nervous? Like, afraid?" I ask. "Are you afraid of me?" My stomach sickens. Over Thanksgiving, Teddy Little, the tight end on the football team, beat up one of Violet's sorority sisters. Penny, I think her name is. Red hair. The whole thing horrified all of us. Most girls are smaller than I am, but I had never truly considered what that must feel like until that happened.

"God, no." Her eyes widen, and her shock eases me. "You're obviously big and strong and..." She blushes, waving her hand over me. "Whatever. But no. Not hurt me." She inhales and meets my gaze. "I'm attracted to you."

She says the words grudgingly, like they're a confession she's making or something she's accusing me of. She holds eye contact, though. There's only honesty there.

All I can do is blink at her. She's attracted to me. That makes the caveman in me roar in approval. She made that 'no funny business' comment yesterday, and I assumed she was reacting to my reputation, not to me. But she's obviously not pleased about the situation. Women have told me they think I'm good-looking before, but it's always coy or flirtatious. Not like this—she doesn't want to find me attractive.

I don't know what to do with that, so I shift into damage-control mode. Right now, this is affecting our dancing. Nothing can get in the way of us winning this thing. Not only that, but I hate that she's uncomfortable. It bothers me, and I need to fix it.

"And…" I prod her, searching for more information to repair what's wrong.

"And?" Her forehead crinkles into an incredulous look. "I'm fairly certain I was explicitly clear."

I wrack my brain for some way to defuse this. "I mean… okay, you think I'm attractive. I think you're hot too." Maybe if she knows that, it won't be as weird for her. Besides, it's the truth.

"You think I'm hot." It's not a question. It's like she's repeating me to clarify.

"Of course." I allow my gaze to sweep over her. I do my best to keep it clinical, like her gorgeous body is a fact, not something that we need to skirt around or something that affects me as much as it does. "Have you looked at you?" I scan her face, and I allow myself to run a finger along her cheek. I force myself to drop the touch, though, before I get carried away and completely freak her out. "Your eyes are so expressive, and they tilt up on the sides. Your lips are so full, I want to nibble at them. You'd almost be too perfect except for your chin." I tap it. "It's pointy, and it's got that cleft in it." I grin at her. "Should have known you'd be stubborn. But you make that look good, too." I step back, making myself put some space between us. "Christ, Ivy." I'm trying to keep this light, but my voice is too husky. "You're gorgeous." I've told girls I think they're pretty before, but this feels different, somehow.

"Thank you?" The words come out like a question, and she looks so confused. The complete expression on her face is adorable, and I need to resist the urge to reach for her.

"You're welcome." Everything I said is completely true.

She stares up at me, her gray eyes swallowing her face like she's shell-shocked.

I'm left scrambling for how to manage this situation.

"That doesn't make you... uncomfortable?"

"Uncomfortable" isn't the right word. Hot and bothered, maybe. Completely turned on. When my skin touches hers, when my body rubs against her, the contact vibrates through me. I'm practically desperate with wanting her. "No. Not uncomfortable." I force myself to shrug. "We're young, and we like the way the other looks. What does that have to do with our dancing?"

"Well..." Her gaze flickers around the room.

I fold my arms across my chest. I try to sound objective and keep this completely professional. "You already said that you want nothing to happen between us, so it won't." It's a good reminder, and I purposefully ignore the wave of disappointment that laces through me. "And that's fine," I add, more for myself than for her. Then inspiration strikes me. "If anything, it's perfect for our performances."

"You think that this will make for good... performance?" She looks mortified.

"Yeah." I gesture between us. "It's almost clichéd, you know? Me, the bad boy with the wicked grin that has girls falling at his feet when I walk by, and you, the good girl who always does the right thing, who has been warned about guys like me. It's a great dynamic." I sure as hell hope I'm right because it hasn't helped me keep her friend-zoned in my head.

"Right." Her smile is too bright. "I hadn't thought of that, but you're right." She waves her hand, all light and breezy, and even though she's just following my lead, I hate how she's writing off what's between us. It doesn't feel right. "Though I don't think I'd go as far as girls falling at your feet when you walk by."

She attempts a teasing grin, so I press a hand against my chest in mock seriousness. "You have no idea. Just swooning, left and right. It's really inconvenient."

"I bet." Her smile is genuine this time, and it loosens the tightness in my chest. "A real tripping hazard."

"Right? Like speed bumps." I laugh. When she's just being herself, Ivy cracks me up. "You don't need to worry, Ivy. You and me?" I wave a hand between us. "We aren't a good match. Look at you." I give her a wink. "You're gorgeous, smart, obviously driven. Even I can tell you're one of the best dancers in the performing arts department. You're beautiful and sweet. Me?" I open my arms wide. "I'm a one-night stand, two if they're lucky. An adrenaline junkie who hopes to make a living pushing a puck along the ice. Unless you're looking for a little fun, I'm not something to be messing around with."

I hate how true all of that is. Because staring into her eyes, I wonder what it would be like to be different. But I'm trying so hard to be someone my team can rely on; someone my family can rely on. I'm not even sure I'm doing that well. There's no way I would take a chance with Ivy.

"But this can be fun, Ivy." I squeeze her hand. "And we can be friends."

Her fingers feel amazing in mine, just like every other time. "Friends."

"Yeah." I shrug. "You know, friends. People who hang out together. I'm actually a lot of fun to be around."

She laughs at him. "Super humble too."

"Please." I blow a raspberry and roll my eyes. "Who has time for that? And now that we've defined our relationship,"— I make exaggerated air quotes—"we can get to work."

Ivy

AFTER THAT TALK, THINGS improve with our dance. Not because I get any less aware of him, because that's definitely not it. If anything, I can feel every touch down to the center of myself. It's made me breathless and achy. But I can't figure out any other way—we're dancing, and it's physical. My body is going to rub against his, and I'm obviously incapable of acting like he doesn't affect me.

Instead, I follow Declan's lead and embrace it. He's right— if we can't avoid being attracted to each other, we might as well give in to it. As he said, that doesn't mean that anything needs to happen.

If I'm honest, it's a relief not to have to pretend. Because now that I don't have to worry about him finding out that I find him attractive, I can just enjoy the way his body makes mine feel alive.

As we twirl around, laughing, and I relish every time his fingers meet my skin, I wonder what it would be like to be the girl he described—the kind of girl who had one-night stands. The girl who could just enjoy being in the moment and not make too much out of it. It's kind of hard, though, for a girl who's never slept with anyone at all to not make a big deal out of sex.

I kind of can't believe I ever thought that anything I'm feeling for Declan would make a difference to someone like him. He's probably heard a million girls prettier and more experienced than me tell him he's hot, both with and without their clothes on. His hotness is a fact of life, and he's used to girls throwing themselves at him. If half of the stuff I heard about him before I left school is true, then he certainly partakes in whatever they offer him—and that was a year ago. I'm sure he's even more experienced now.

He's right. We're complete opposites. He's the local hockey bimbo, and I'm still a virgin at twenty-one. Even before I got sick, I wasn't a casual fling kind of girl. Now, I'm certain I couldn't manage one, especially not with someone like him.

I check the time after another run-through of our dance. I must admit, things got much better in the second half of practice. Clearing the air helped. "That's all our time for today." I furrow my brows. "I don't suppose you'll have time tomorrow?"

He shakes his head. "It's game day, our last one, before we have two weeks off for the holiday."

"Oh." I won't see him for two weeks. I hate that I'm disappointed about that.

"When do you leave for the break?"

"I was going to drive home on Saturday if I could get another day of practice in tomorrow." I shrug. "But if you aren't available, I guess I'll just go home early." I've been enjoying the freedom of being away from my family and back on my own. I'm excited to spend the holidays with my parents because I adore them, but after the year I've had, it's decadent to feel... normal.

"Don't go home early. If you don't have plans, why don't you come to the hockey game tomorrow night? We always party after the games. I'll introduce you to some of my friends."

"I don't know..." I reach for my towel. "You're busy. It's not a big deal. I don't want to put you out."

He reaches into his bag, snags his phone, then taps on the screen for a few seconds. "It's done. I forwarded you the ticket for my seat in the team section."

"What?" I glare at him. "I didn't even agree to go yet."

"You were going to," he offers with complete confidence. He's right, but that doesn't mean he needs to rub it in. "Besides, this way I can introduce you to two of my friends." He pauses and enunciates, "Girl friends."

"Not only aren't you humble, but you're also incredibly overbearing." I mean it to come out heated, but it doesn't.

"Yep." Totally unrepentant. "Shea Carmichael and Violet Tannehill. They're great."

"How do you know that we'll like each other?" As much as I hate to admit it, I don't know that many people on campus. When I was here before, I spent most of my time with the other dance majors. Most of the people I've stayed in touch with aren't on campus now that finals are over, so it's been an awkward return.

"I understand people, Princess. I got this." He's so confident that I instinctively trust his judgment. He tosses his phone back into his bag.

"Are you always so self-assured?"

"No." He grins. He says nothing else, and that makes me laugh.

"No?"

"No one knows what they're doing all the time." The layers of swagger that Declan wraps himself in slip, and for a second, he looks open and honest, almost vulnerable. He shrugs. "But I am serious about our performance. The second half of that dance... I really think we can be great. And even if we're opposites and aren't a good fit in real life, the people in the audience don't have to know that."

I swallow, drowning in the intensity of his deep brown eyes. "You're right." And he is, about all of it. We aren't a good fit in real life, him with all his confidence and sexuality, and me still trying to string together the broken pieces of myself.

But I can't help wondering what it would be like to be the kind of girl that Declan Mitchell got close to.

Declan

I'M MORE NERVOUS FOR Ivy to show up for the game than I was before prom.

We're hosting State, and it's a great matchup for her to see. They play hard, but this year, they can't keep up with us. I don't want to examine why I really want to win in front of her.

"Mitch." Ash, my third roommate, hangs out of the locker room door, interrupting my staring down the hall and waiting for her to appear.

"Hey. What's up?" As before every game, Ash looks like he's ready to vomit.

"The guys are almost ready." I nod. Part of my pregame routine is going around to each of the guys in the locker room and saying hello.

"What are you doing out here?"

I crane my neck as another couple comes down the hallway. Not her. "Just waiting for someone." Finally, I spot Ivy as she rounds the corner, and I can't help but smile. "I'll be right in."

Ash follows my gaze and raises his brows. "Just someone?"

"It's not like that. She's my dance partner in that dance competition. She's a sweet girl."

"Ah." He nods, and I'm not certain but he appears to approve. "What's her name?"

"Ivy. I'm going to introduce her to Shea and Violet."

He wrinkles his brows in question.

I shrug it off. "She's been off campus for a while, and she said a lot of her friends have left for the semester."

He nods, watching her head toward me. Instead of the leggings or tights that she usually wears, she's got on a pair of jeans that hug her in all the right places. She's wearing a winter coat, which is good. It's cold in the rink, especially as close to the ice as she'll be sitting.

Her short hair is a mass of waves on her head, and she looks fucking gorgeous, which is completely fine. I'm a red-blooded man, and I appreciate beautiful women. That's basically what I told her yesterday. But I left parts out because it was the right thing to do and because there shouldn't be anything between us except dancing.

I need to ignore how much the animation in her eyes holds me captive, and I definitely need to stop looking forward to seeing her so much. But most of all, I need to stop wanting her so fucking bad.

Lots of people—guys and girls—think I'm an arrogant prick. Hell, I've got a healthy ego, no doubt. I'm a smart guy, and I notice how women look at me. But what they don't get is that most of the comments I make are self-deprecating. I'm not a fool. I understand that the first thing anyone notices about another person is their appearance. I know also that despite being kind of a goofy-looking middle-school kid, I've matured into someone women like to look at. But that middle-school boy inside me who barely remembered to comb his hair still thinks it's hysterical that girls hit on him all the time.

Except all I keep thinking about is Ivy telling me she thinks I'm attractive. It kept me up last night.

"Hey," she says when she joins me, her hands tucked in her pockets. She's five and a half feet, so Ash and I tower over her in our skates. She wrinkles her nose. "Ew. What's that smell?"

I point behind us. "Locker room."

"I can smell it all the way out here?" She pinches her lips together, and I stifle my laughter. Like the rest of the guys, I'm so used to the stench that I don't even notice it anymore.

"Yeah." I waggle my eyebrows at her. "Pretty good, huh?" I puff up, pretending to be proud.

She waves her hand in front of her face. "Gross. I thought my pointe shoes smelled bad."

"You hurt our feelings, Princess. That's the smell of paragons of masculinity, all marinating in their own masculine masculine-ness." The smile on my face almost hurts. I can't get enough of going back and forth with her.

"That's a lot of masculine masculinity, then." She grins as she glances over my shoulder, then rocks back and forth on her heels. "So... thanks for inviting me." She looks at Ash.

Damn it, I almost forgot he was here. I glare at him, wishing he had gone somewhere else. Begrudgingly, I wave over him and introduce them. "Ivy Deveraux, this is Ash Draper, one of my roommates and the center on my line. Nosy too. Like someone's grandma."

He gives a nod. "I'd shake your hand, but I was just wearing my gloves." He wrinkles his nose. "Pretty sure gloves account for most hockey stink."

"You sure?" I say, raising my eyebrows at him. Is he really hitting on my girl after I just told him she was off-limits?

He nods solemnly. "Absolutely."

"I've smelled your hockey equipment. I don't think your assessment is correct."

Laughing, Ivy nods back at him. "Nice to meet you."

When Ash doesn't move quickly enough to leave, I scowl at him. *God, he's nosy.* "Tell the guys I'll be right in. I'm just going to show her to her seat." I motion for Ivy to go in front of me, and she walks ahead, toward the stands. I glance back, and Ash makes smooching faces at me, so I give him the finger and shoo him along.

I shake my head even as I smother a grin. It's not like that, though. We're friends. That's all. I need to keep repeating that in my head.

I trudge awkwardly after her in my skate guards. At the end of the tunnel, I stop her. "Okay, this is our section. Hold on." I step up onto the stairs, balancing on my skate guards. I texted Shea earlier that I was going to be bringing someone, so I'm sure she's looking for me, if only out of straight-up curiosity.

Sure enough, she waves at me and heads down the stairs, her long brown hair on her shoulders. She's not fast, thanks to the obscene heels on her boots. Then again, I rarely see her in anything that's not high. She's tiny, though, especially next to Linc, her boyfriend, who's one of the tallest guys on the team. She probably doesn't want to get a crick in her neck when she hugs him.

"Declan, hey. This must be Ivy." Shea turns her warm gaze on Ivy, sticking out her hand. "I'm Shea Carmichael. I've known the guys for years, and Linc, one of Declan's roommates, is my boyfriend."

Ivy takes that in and nods before shaking Shea's hand and offering her a cautious smile. "Hi. I'm Ivy Deveraux." She squares her shoulders and returns her gray gaze to me. "I got this. You've got a game to play or something, right?"

Watching the two of them interact, I'm glad that I invited Ivy. Shea's a doll, and Violet's a trip. They'll keep an eye on her.

"I don't just play this game, sweetheart. I dominate it."

Both Ivy and Shea roll their eyes, and I smother a grin.

Yeah, they're going to get on fine. I wink at them. "I'll see you after the game, pretty ladies. Have fun."

I watch as Ivy goes up to the seats with Shea, and Shea introduces her to Violet. If I watch any longer, I'm going to look like a stalker, so I turn and head back toward the locker room.

My face splits into a huge grin as I enter the space. It really does stink in here.

"Yo, Hunter." I slap the other winger on my line on the shoulder. "You ready?" Hunter's a great guy. Quiet, though. Keeps to himself.

He nudges his head at me, his eyes narrowing. "Bet I'll get more than you, Mitch."

"Not on the ice or off it, pal."

Hunter shakes his head, chuckling.

I move on to the next guy. This is the part of being captain I really enjoy. I make my way around the locker room, equal parts pep talking and calming guys, whatever they need. By the time the emcee calls our team and we hit the ice to a roar of cheers, I have a pretty good idea of how everyone's doing, which is why I snag Griff's sleeve on the way to the bench. "Wyatt's wound tight. Keep an eye on him."

Wyatt is the sophomore who's starting tonight on defense with Griff, taking Linc's spot until Linc's groin pull heals and he's cleared to play. "He's got the burn in him, but if he doesn't settle…"

"Got it, Mitch," he says with a nod, skating off to check on the rookie.

Everyone else seems set, so I take a second to glance at the stands where Ivy's sitting. When I see her looking at me, I salute her. I'm not sure, but I think she shakes her head and rolls her eyes. That has me chuckling as I drop my spare stick on the bench and head to the center of the ice for face-off.

But I can't deny how much I like having her here, watching me.

I take a deep breath, the puck drops, and it's game on.

Ivy

I DIDN'T ADMIT IT to Declan, but I actually know a few things about hockey. My father's law firm has a box at Madison Square Garden, and he's taken me to a few games to watch the Rangers play. Dad's a fan of the sport, but more than that, he enjoys knowing more about everything than anyone else, so every time I went with him, he regaled me with details about the game, its strategies, and its traditions.

I know that Declan's a forward based on where he lines up for face-offs. Left wing, if I'm not mistaken. He's also as fast as the NHL players I've seen, which makes sense. NHL teams have drafted some of these guys and they'll play for them some day. If they don't play at that level, maybe they'll be in the minors for a while. My father was sure to point out when I accepted a place at Chesterboro that the hockey team was division one. The only other sport here with that designation is the football team.

I assumed Declan would be good, but I didn't know how good. He doesn't disappoint. He's fast, naturally graceful, and skates with the same sort of volatile energy that I recognize from our dancing.

I've heard he's unpredictable on the ice. He's quick, but he's also dynamic. He doesn't make some plays that are expected from his position. That might not be a bad thing, exactly, at least not all the time. Mostly, Ash and his other linesman, Hunter Mason, seem to read his mind, probably thanks to being line mates with him for a while now.

As Ash misreads Declan's pass, I ask Shea, "How long have the three of them been on a line together?"

"Their first year," she says while watching Linc send a pass up the boards to Hunter, who breaks out. Declan stays to the middle, skating directly at the net. Shea cheers as a two-on-one develops. The lone State defenseman commits to following Hunter, who quickly passes the puck to Declan. Declan doesn't even take a moment to receive it before ripping off a slapshot at the goalie. The puck sails over the goalie's shoulder, glove side, lighting the lamp behind his net.

Shea, Violet, the rest of our section, and I explode into cheers along with the rest of our section as Declan celebrates on the ice with his teammates. As he skates along the bench, slapping his glove against each of his teammates', they bang their sticks against the board. The emcee announces his goal, and I clap, my cheeks hurting from smiling at him.

From this close to the ice, I can see his face, and his gaze finds mine. He's so happy. It's easy to read even from my seat. But it's not only happiness—he looks alive.

It should scare me, all that energy in him. It's raw and magnetic, though, and I can't help but be drawn to that. I want to feel like that again. I'm sure, in the past, I did. I loved to dance. I loved to live. I want that back, and being around him reminds me of how that feels.

I watch as Declan makes another unexpected play, only this time, the puck doesn't end up in the net. In fact, because he's out of position, the defender snags it. He passes it forward, and it ends up as a breakaway toward our goalie. Luckily, our goalie is on top of his game, and he makes the save, stopping play.

"He makes some impulsive plays," I comment. It seems that there would have been safer options.

Shea answers with her eyes still on her boyfriend, who is skating backward with the other team's winger. "Always. Last year, he had Cord to keep him in check, but this year, he's the captain. He's supposed to be the one keeping everyone else in line."

As far as I can tell, Declan's a chaos agent. "How's that going?"

"When he's on, the rest of the team follows suit. When he isn't…" She shrugs.

I understand what she means. I wonder how that translates in the locker room.

The game progresses, and we stay up by one point the whole time. In the last period, the State team puts up more of a fight, but they're no match for our momentum. We win, 4-3.

I cheer along with the rest of the spectators as Declan celebrates with his team.

I skip down the stairs after my new friends, excited to see him. I chat with the girls in the hallway while the guys shower. He steps out of the locker room, hair still wet, his eyes glowing, and my heart skips in my chest, heat racing along my skin. When he sees me, his grin widens, and it hits me I'm not just attracted to Declan—I want him.

I drop my gaze as if he is going to see the realization in my eyes. But I catch myself—that's ridiculous. Still, I'm flushed and warm and completely off-balance when he wraps his arm around my shoulder. "Hey there, Princess. How did you like the game?"

"Fishing for compliments?" I ask, doing my best to pull myself out of my head and back into the friendship that we agreed to.

"Always." He squeezes me. When I don't smile back, a wrinkle forms between his brows. "What's up? You okay?"

I force a grin. "Absolutely. Congratulations on the win."

"Thanks." He drops his arm, though. He's probably reading my mood, so I inhale and attempt a more convincing smile.

"I'm good. Come on, we have a party to get to." I loop my arm through his, and we set off like friends because that's what we're supposed to be.

Declan

THE PARTY AFTER OUR win is at Shepherd Hall, like most of our post-game celebrations, but this one is low key. Most of the student population has gone home for winter break, so it's mostly the team and a few other people who are stuck on campus for clubs or for other sports.

Shea is still here because she's driving home tomorrow with Linc. He's going to drop her at her parents' house in New York City before heading to Long Island, where they both grew up. Linc's excited to see his mother. She recently started a new treatment for her multiple sclerosis and appears to be doing well. Since Shea's family plans to stay in the city for the holiday, they'll be doing a lot of commuting. They invited me in for a New Year's Eve party. I need to see how things play out with my father, Pam, and Stephen first.

Violet's still around because her flight home to Texas doesn't leave until tomorrow night.

That's all fine with me. The chill vibe gives me an opportunity to play a game that I love and excel at: beer pong.

"What do you mean, you've never played beer pong?" I ask Ivy, tossing a ping-pong ball up in the air and catching it in my hand.

"Just that. I've seen it played, but usually I dance at parties."
She shrugs.

"Then you are in the right place, Princess, because you can learn from a master of the game." I puff up my chest and stay straight-faced, but Griff snorts across the table. "A couple things. Lots of people throw underhand, but that's not good control. It's better to throw overhand, like this." I demonstrate, pinching the ball between my index finger and my thumb. "I find it's easiest to aim at one of the red cups. Then you try to sink the ball."

"This doesn't sound difficult." She eyes the table skeptically.

"Well, if the opposing team sinks a ball into your cup, you need to drink the beer in the cup." Violet tilts the front cup over to show the contents. "We only filled them up a little, though. Everyone's got to travel tomorrow."

Ivy tilts her head up to me, wrinkling her adorable nose. "I hate beer."

"Suck it up, buttercup. There's not a lot in there."

She sticks her tongue out at me, and the sight of it against her lips does unwanted things to my dick. I lean closer. "Did you want to sit this out? I can get someone else to play if you're not up to it." I mean it as a real get-out-of-jail-free card, but I should have known better.

Her eyes flash with a competitive gleam. "No way, Mitchell. Let's do this."

What follows is a lot of laughing, competitive heckling, and general ball-busting. I wasn't sure that Ivy was going to get into the game, but she does. She figures it out pretty fast, which doesn't surprise me. To be fair, it's not complicated.

Drunk people play it. But she likes to win almost as much as I do.

This is exactly the atmosphere that I wanted for her tonight. She's having fun here with me, I'm sure of it. She's horsing around with everyone else, her eyes alive.

The more time I spend with her, the more I genuinely like her. I tell myself that's good because it's important for our dancing that she sees we can actually be friends. But deep down, I know that's bullshit. It isn't only about the dance. And I don't just think she's fun to be around either.

I can't stop looking at her.

Before long, we've won three games and lost two. The amount of beer that Violet put in the cups isn't anything to me, but for a tiny thing like Ivy, it's taking a toll. I offer to drink a couple of them, but she takes it as a personal affront before tipping the last one back and chugging.

She wrinkles her nose, as she has after every drink she's taken. This time, she even shivers. "Yucky."

A vision of her from a year ago fills my brain, her long hair trailing down her back as she chugged a cup of whatever cheap shit we'd bought for that party. I even remember that she covered her mouth to keep from burping. The memory makes me grin. "I remember you said something almost exactly like that last year." I'm not sure if I should bring it up, but we're having such a good time. I keep hoping that whatever defensiveness she felt before is gone now.

She drops the cup into the stack of empties next to us. "It's still true."

I reach up to tweak one curl on her head. "Your hair was super long back then. I love this, though. Why did you decide to cut it all off?"

She goes completely still, and her eyes widen. In the week I've known her, I've watched her tense when we dance, and I've seen her irritated. I've witnessed a handful of other emotions play across her face as well, ones that I haven't quite defined yet. This, though, is completely different. Whatever this emotion is, I hate it.

She drops her face, tucking a strand behind her ear. Except her hair's not long enough to tuck, really, so it comes off more like a nervous habit than anything else. "It was time."

What the hell does that mean? I stare at her.

"Hey, Ivy. Your shot," Griff calls from across the table.

As I watch, she squares her shoulders and raises her head. The smile on her lips is too bright, and she holds up the ping pong ball and hands it to me. "Here. You take my shot. I'm going to run outside and get some air. I'll be right back." She spins on her heels and strides out of the room.

Shit. Whatever just happened, it was a major fuckup on my part. Wide-eyed, I glance at Griff and Ash as if they have the answers. Ash shakes his head, and Griff can only shrug. Right —they wouldn't have any idea either.

Hurrying, I quickly grab the last two cups, chug their contents, and take off after her. Over my shoulder, I call to Hunter, "Mason, you're up on the table."

The entire process takes ten seconds. Because my legs are so much longer than Ivy's, I catch up with her on the porch. "Hey," I call to her, but she doesn't stop. I snag her arm, pulling her to a stop. "Ivy, hey. Wait up." I run my hand over my hair. I didn't take the time to comb it after my shower, so it's falling in my eyes. "I'm sorry. Whatever I said to upset you."

She inhales, glancing up at the sky. She pastes a polite smile on her face. "I think I'm going to head back to my room. I'm supposed to be getting back to the city in the morning. It's a long drive."

I pop my hands on my hips. "Seriously. I just apologized. Aren't you going to acknowledge that?" When she only stares at me, I sigh. "Okay, I guess not. Well, why don't we go back inside? We can do something else." She says nothing, so I glance around. "Or we can stay right here, on the porch. Just hang out. Chat."

"Why are you trying this hard to be nice to me?" The question is full of exasperation.

"Honestly, I have no idea," I snap back at her. "You're kind of prickly and unpredictable. And for me to call someone unpredictable... well, that's something." I immediately feel bad. She doesn't need to explain anything to me. I'm not her boyfriend. I'm supposed to be her friend, and if I actually plan to be her friend, I should act like it and give her space. I exhale a calming breath and try a smile. "You know what? No problem. I get it. Travel. But I'm still sorry if I upset you. Have a great break." I head for the door because I'm sure she doesn't want me standing there, looking at her.

"Damn it, Declan. Wait."

I pause, turning back slowly, as if she's an animal I might spook. It's close to the truth because once again, I'm out of my element with her.

"You're right. That was an irrational response, which probably made absolutely no sense to you because it barely made sense to me." She sighs. "It's just... I'm still a little sensitive about my hair, okay?"

Sensitive about her hair? I reach for something witty, something that's going to diffuse whatever heaviness that's suddenly fallen on this conversation. "Bad haircuts, they're—"

"I had to shave it off. Last year, right after I started chemotherapy." She runs a hand over it, and the soft curls bounce back. "It started falling out in clumps, and some people told me that I should just let whatever happens happen, but that felt so... out of control, and I couldn't feel like that. So, I had my mom shave it all off one night."

A rushing sound fills my ears. "Chemotherapy."

"Yeah. Chemotherapy." She must have grabbed her jacket from next to the door on her way out because she zips it up and tucks her hands in her pockets. "For Hodgkin's lymphoma."

I'm never speechless. It's a blessing and a curse. Most of the time, I can figure out what I'm supposed to say in any situation. Sometimes, though, it means that I say too much when I should just stop talking. Growing up, my mouth got me into lots of trouble.

But right now, looking into the beautiful, stubborn face of one of the most talented and physically fit people I've met in a long time, I don't know what to say. When I'd been wondering where she'd gone last year, why I couldn't find her, I expected nothing like this. I never expected that she might have gone home to fight for her life.

"Right." She rocks back and forth on her feet. "That one always goes over great at parties. I have to figure out how to tell that story better, I think." She points at the stairs and takes a step toward them. "So... cool. Okay, then. I'll just text you. Over break. Have a great holiday."

In two steps, I reach for her, tugging her into my arms. I'm not sure which one of us is more surprised that she meets my hug willingly. Either way, she steps closer, leaning into me, and I fold my arms around her.

I'm a hugger, and if anyone needs a hug right now, it's Ivy.

We stand there like that for long seconds. It's definitely long enough for me to realize a few things. First, this is not a thing she wants to talk about. If she did, it wouldn't have been so painful for her to say, and she wouldn't have been so uncomfortable about it. She could have just said something back at the beer pong table and played it off. But she didn't. That means that any of the questions I have—when, how bad, how are you—need to stay with me. I've been asked stuff I don't want to talk about lots of times, and it doesn't feel good.

The second, more pressing thing I notice is that Ivy Deveraux still fits perfectly against my body. Sure, we've been dancing together for the past few days, and I've dipped her, held her hands, all that stuff. But this is different. She's curled into me, and the way she feels is so exquisite, it sucks the breath out of my lungs. I have held more women than I care to admit, but this is much, much different.

She tenses, though, so I force myself to let her step away. It's one thing to be a hugger and another thing completely to be a too-long hugger, especially with someone who's supposed to be a friend. She glances up at me, uncertainty and questions in her brown eyes.

This situation could get very over-serious quickly, and that's definitely not what she wants. So, I clear my throat. "Thanks," I say. "Whew, I needed a hug." The incredulous look she gives me is exactly the reaction I was going for. I raise a shoulder. "What? I'm extremely sensitive."

She cracks up, and I breathe a sigh of relief. She's laughing, so everything is going to be all right. If I can get a girl laughing, I can fix anything. That's a lesson I learned from my dear old man. His exact sentiment was "if you can get a girl to laugh, you can get in her pants." He might be even more of a man-whore than I am, but the idea is the same. Laughter makes everyone more comfortable.

"You know what else I need?" I ask.

She cocks her head to the side.

"Fried food."

She furrows her brows. "It's one in the morning, Declan."

"Right." I pull out my phone, pulling up my food delivery app. "Fried food and a hoagie."

She huffs out another laugh, but her eyes sparkle in the porch light. "Where does one get something like that this late?"

I place my hand on my chest. "Please tell me you've had Creative Deli before?"

"The place next to that gas station on Clifford Street?" She shakes her head. "They have food?"

There's no way that a senior at Chesterboro hasn't had food from CD. "That's it. I'm not getting delivery. We're going right now. You up for a walk, Princess?"

I half expect her to say no. I would understand. But she tilts her head, tucks her hands back into her pockets, and grins at me. "Sure. Why not?"

Ivy

"BUT DO YOU LIKE mushrooms?" The answer to this question seems very important to Declan.

"Sure. They're fine."

We wait next to the counter at Creative Deli while the poor night-shift worker makes the food we just ordered. I wasn't lying—I've never been in CD, but I've heard of it. It's not really a place that the dancers in my program frequent. It mostly sells vaping paraphernalia, cigarettes, and food that's the equivalent of a late-night hookup—great at the moment but something to regret in the morning.

He considers. "Most people have powerful feelings about mushrooms. Either they like them, or they really dislike them."

"I'm not most people."

"True enough." He glances at the pools of grease in the back where the half-asleep cook tossed his mushrooms earlier. "You're in for a treat, though. Fried mushrooms are delicious."

I hypothesize that anything you eat after drinking late at night is probably delicious. It's almost two in the morning. The delicatessen is empty except for us. The only other customer I've seen was a guy who ran in to buy smokes a few minutes after we got here. The place is probably booming during the day, but now, with the night pressing against the windows, it's quiet, almost intimate.

I try not to think about that with Declan standing next to me, but I can't help it. I've told myself at least a dozen times this evening—maybe two dozen—that we're only friends. My body is ignoring me, though. What's worse is that I wish it was only because I find him insanely attractive. But that's not it.

I like him so much.

Declan chatted the entire walk here, asking a bunch of questions about my favorite types of foods and a hundred other things. He's so easy to talk to. What surprises me is that he doesn't ask the questions about cancer that I expect. At first, I was glad. I've been awkward before, but telling him I had been sick on the porch might be my crowning achievement. Extending the social clumsiness would have been painful.

As we started walking and that dissipated, though, I realized that talking about it would have been okay. At least with him.

Now, he falls into companionable silence. It's so strange that he's quiet that I glance up at him. As always, he appears completely at ease.

I wish I could say the same.

Coming back to school after a year, I knew I would need to talk about being sick. It's not a dirty secret I'm keeping. I talked with other survivors about how they handled it. My friend Jessie said she started a lot of conversations for the first year in remission with, "Hi, I'm Jessie, and I had cancer." She said it was easier just to put it out there than to have people wonder about gaps at school or her scars, a kind of offense-is-the-best-defense mentality. But I don't want to lead conversations with it. It's not who I am—it's something that happened to me.

Another girl said that she just ignored the looks and didn't bring it up, but if people asked about it, she'd talk about it. She said that it's not her business what others think of her—it's theirs. I wish I was that confident. But I'm not.

Humans are uncomfortable around things they fear, and most people are afraid of life-threatening illness. I told myself I'd figure it out when I got there, that when the subject came up, it would be natural to talk about it. But it's not. How do I explain any of it? A year of treatments, of worry, of hope and dread—sometimes in the same day—and the weight of other people's pity. Or worse, other people's assumptions—that somehow because I was going through chemotherapy and radiation, I was naturally fearless and brave when often I was just terrified.

There are no good words for all of that. I didn't need to explain, though. At least not to Declan. He just pulled me into his arms and hugged me. It was perfect. He didn't push or ask a bunch of questions, and not one trace of pity showed on his face.

I cast a sideways glance at him as we wait.

He doesn't even look at me when he asks, "What?"

"Why didn't you ask any questions?"

"Did you want me to?" He watches the deli worker lift the basket out of the grease and shake it, rubbing his hands together. "Perfection." The guy tosses Declan's fried mushrooms onto a paper-lined tray and shakes them again. The entire process fills me with equal parts fascination and horror. They smell amazing, but I can't shake the knowledge that they're probably the most fattening, artery-clogging thing I might ever eat.

"If you fry them, doesn't that remove every possible health benefit of the vegetable?"

"They're not technically vegetables, you know. They're part of the fungi kingdom."

"Okay…"

"Did you know that there's actually a lot of protein in mushrooms?" He accepts the takeout container of his mushrooms and the one with the gravy fries I requested from the worker and a bag holding his foot-long hoagie. There's enough food here for four people. "Lots of other vitamins, too. Well, not these. You're right—frying them ruins most of their nutritional value. But in general." He meets my questioning gaze. "Biology major."

"You are?" I always assumed most of the jocks at school took easy majors, or at least majors that they could bullshit their way through. Biology doesn't sound like that kind of major.

"Yep. Love to study how things work." I don't know him well yet, but that dovetails with everything I know about him. He motions toward the door. "I know the perfect place to eat this stuff."

Outside, we head back toward campus. I've got our drinks tucked under my arm—sports drink for him, water for me. It's late, and I'm sleepy, but I don't want to leave his company. For a guy so full of energy, he's surprisingly easy to be with.

We cut through the quad, weaving along the path under the lamps. Finally, he stops in front of the stairs to the South Hall. "Here."

I look around. "Here?"

He nods, sliding forward to sit on the stone stairs of the building. He pats the step next to him. "Come on. This heart attack isn't going to eat itself."

I do as he asks, lowering myself next to him. He hands me the container with my fries in them, and I open it. The smell of gravy hits my nose, and I sigh. "I don't let myself eat this stuff very often."

"Yeah?" He opens the mushrooms and sighs happily. "Me either, really. But as far as I'm concerned, the holidays start now. I plan to eat my face off for the next two weeks and suffer the consequences after the new year." He opens the lid on the sauce that came with his deep-fried fungus. "Horseradish sauce."

"With mushrooms?"

He hums his happiness. "Oh, you wait." He holds the whole thing out to me. "You first. Watch it, though. They're probably still hot on the inside. I suggest dipping, then letting it sit for a second."

I do as he requests. While I wait, he unwraps his hoagie and dives in, so I snag a few fries, slide them through the extra gravy, and pop the mess in my mouth.

I can't help it—I moan. I haven't had a French fry in months. At the height of my sickness, I had little appetite, so I ate whatever I was in the mood for. Most of the time, it didn't taste that good, no matter what it was. After I felt better, I started working out more, preparing to get back to dance. That meant not indulging in junk food as much.

I catch him staring at me, his hoagie halfway to his mouth. "What?" I ask.

"That's not a sound I usually hear outside of the bedroom, Princess." His eyes are half-lidded, his gaze fixed on my mouth.

My face heats, and I need to break the eye contact. I can't think about Declan in a bedroom. Fine, I can picture it perfectly in my head, at least what I think it would look like. His tattoos, the nipple ring... his perfect backside and thighs. His shaggy hair and the bedroom eyes he's giving me right now.

But this is Declan—he's probably teasing. Even if he isn't, he's been clear about what relationships he has—short and heavy on bedroom antics. That shouldn't make me feel so breathless.

I attempt a laugh, but it's wispy. To distract myself, I grab a few more fries and some more gravy and take another bite.

"Thanks, by the way," I finally say. I manage to glance at him again, and he chews as he casts me a questioning look. "For not being weird at Shepherd."

He swallows his bite of food. "I'm never weird."

My lips tilt up. "Right." I continue eating, the takeout container open in my lap. Offhand, I say, "You're the first person I've told since I got back." I shrug. "My teachers know. The department helped me finish my semester last fall. I could even take two courses remotely, which was very accommodating of them."

"That must have been difficult," he offers after taking a sip of his drink.

"Studying remotely?" I shake my head. "Not at all, actually."

"I mean... taking college classes when you were dealing with cancer." His words are matter-of-fact.

My head snaps up, and I meet his eyes, bracing myself for the worst—the pity. But I find only understanding, sympathy, and respect.

"You probably had a lot going on in your head. Making room for, like, liberal arts credits in the middle of all of that… that must have been hard." He tilts his head, shrugging. "I can barely focus on that shit on a regular day, and I didn't have extenuating circumstances like a life-threatening disease."

I swallow hard, staring at him. If he was anyone else, I might play it down or deflect. But with Declan, it doesn't feel like I can. I don't want to. "Actually, it was nice to have something to take my mind off of it."

He nods, accepting that without question. Offhand, I realize that's another one of Declan's talents—he makes me feel like I can say anything, no matter what it is. If it's the truth, he'll take it. That is incredibly freeing. I've spent the past year holding it together for myself and my family. They asked how I felt, and I would say "fine" or "great" even when it was a lie because it was easier to make them feel better than to be honest.

But I get the impression that Declan would hate that.

We eat in silence for long minutes, then I clear my throat. Time for a less serious conversation. "So, what are your plans for the holidays? You're going home?"

He nods, chewing the last bite of his hoagie. After he swallows, he says, "I'm headed to Brooklyn, to my mom's place. I'll spend until Christmas Eve with her, then I'll spend Christmas day at my father's place in Midtown."

"You'll be in New York?" I wave the last fry in my container, excited. "My parents' place is in Soho. You know what this means?"

"We both need to drive through horrific traffic tomorrow?"

"No." I cock my head. "Well, yes. But also, we can get together and practice our dance over the break."

He groans. "All work and no play, Princess. I thought you were going to propose some sort of romantic interlude or something. A 'what happens in New York stays in New York' kind of thing."

I throw my takeout container in the plastic bag he has and scowl at him. "That's Vegas. And besides, you don't want a romantic interlude with me. Remember?"

I hate that I'm the one pointing this out to him. Because if there's anything I've realized tonight with Declan, it's that I definitely do want him. It's not smart for all the reasons he outlined the other day. He and I are as different as night and day, and I'm supposed to steer clear of guys like him.

Tell that to my stupid body.

He considers. "I did not say that. I said that casual stuff is all I do. Not that I don't want you. You're confusing everything."

I can only blink at that. The way he states he wants me, especially when I want him too… it's short-circuiting my brain, making me think about what it would actually be like to be in his arms, to be touched by him, even if it's only something brief and casual.

None of that is a way to keep this conversation light, though, so I soldier through. "What do you say, Mitchell? You up to get together to practice on vacation or what?"

He appears skeptical. "Do you have somewhere we can do that?"

"I have a studio in my parents' house. You can come there if you'd like." I imagine him in my home, around my things, and excitement washes over me.

"Sounds good. Let me know when." He gathers the rest of our trash, throws it into the bag, and stands. He offers me a hand. "I'll walk you back to your dorm."

I point across the quad to the temporary housing I'm staying in. "It's right there. You don't have to do that."

"I know." He keeps his hand out. I slide my fingers into it, enjoying the warmth of his grasp in the cold. I admit—I revel in every bit of contact between us. "Let's go."

Ivy

BY MONDAY MORNING, I'M already suffocating at home.

"How are you feeling?" My mom peeks her head into my bedroom.

I barely refrain from rolling my eyes at her. I was only at school for a couple of weeks, but the freedom was heavenly.

"I told you, Mom, I'm fine. I feel great. You don't have to stay home from work today to monitor me." When I got back to New York yesterday, my mom mentioned in passing that she planned to take today off. She's an attorney, so that meant that she would need to reschedule appointments. I told her it was unnecessary, that I could be home alone. But she insisted. I gave up trying to convince her. It took her a long time for her to finally leave me by myself in the fall, and it seems that we're back in that same spot. "You do realize that I've enrolled next semester full time, right?" I keep the question light, but I'm serious.

She smiles but looks stricken. "Of course, baby. But it's not too much for a mother to want to see her daughter after she's been gone for two weeks, is it?"

"Of course not," I reassure her. As always, after suggesting she's being too smothering, guilt washes over me. I can't imagine what this must've been like for her. I'm her only child. My cancer happened not only to me—it happened to my family as well. "Hey, do you have plans for lunch?"

We both know she would spend her lunch in her office, working, but she shakes her head. "Absolutely not. Do you want to go out for a bite?"

"I haven't been to Fuji in a while. Sushi sound good?"

My mother's smile reassures me I'm doing the right thing. "Sounds great." Some time, in the months to come, she will stop worrying every time I leave her sight, but we aren't there yet, and I remind myself to be patient with my parents, same as I need to be patient with myself.

She steps into my room, glancing at the computer propped up in front of me. "What are you doing?"

I motion to the screen, where a video of a couple doing the salsa is playing. "Research. I told you about the dance competition, right?" I wait for her to nod. "I was thinking we could do a salsa for a second date."

"Salsa, huh? That's a complicated dance. Are you sure your partner can keep up?"

I glance back at the screen, thinking about it clinically. If anything, I struggle to dance with him. Not because I can't do the steps, but because I'm completely distracted by him. "Absolutely." At my mom's questioning glance, I continue. "He's the captain of the hockey team. Naturally athletic. He's actually more than that. He's a wonderful dancer."

"Is he?" Her eyebrows raise in interest. "And?"

"And what, Mom?" I tease.

She puts her hands on her hips in mock reprimand, and I chuckle.

"I told you. He's a really good dancer." Declan is a lot of things, but I'm not sure I'm ready to talk about any of them. I don't even understand how I feel about a lot of it. "His mom lives in Brooklyn, so we thought we could get together over break and practice here. I thought it would be a good opportunity to get ahead on our planning."

I can see the wheels turning in my mother's mind. "Well, you know, Ivy…" She taps her lips, but she's not fooling me. She's up to something. "The salsa is one of those dances that is hard to understand by watching."

This time, I do roll my eyes at her. "That's why I'm trying to find videos to show him, Mom."

"No, I mean, really watching." She puts a hand on her stomach and one up in the air like they do in the movies when they pretend to dance with other people. She shimmies around my room. "You need to go somewhere to feel the rhythm. To hear the music. To be in it."

I narrow my eyes at her. "What exactly are you trying to say here?"

She sighs. "You're not good at this, are you? There are a lot of good salsa clubs in town. Find one. Have him meet you there. Take him out."

"I don't know. We're just friends." I can hear my disappointment in my voice.

"Great," she says. "Even better. That way, I don't have to worry about you." She plops down on the bed next to me and gives me a sideways squeeze. "Go out, baby. Have fun. Go dancing like a regular person, not just because it's for work. If it's with a cute guy, even better."

"I didn't say he was cute, Mom."

"You didn't have to, Ivy." She grins. "I know you. The way you said he was a wonderful dancer…" She presses the back of her hand against her forehead and pretends to swoon. I laugh at her. "If you're just friends, that's fine. Just go. Have fun."

It's a little frustrating how everyone has been telling me to have fun. They make me sound like a crotchety old woman. But my mother isn't entirely wrong. The last year or so… it's not just that it wasn't fun, it's that I couldn't be there, not truly present. I spent the time surviving, worrying about the future. But even that story leaves out the details. We had holidays, but worries and fears overshadowed them. I didn't date. Not that I dated much before I got sick, but I definitely didn't date afterward.

My mother is telling me to go be young. For her, this isn't about Declan. It's another step in proving that I'm truly better, that I'm not sick anymore.

But it makes me wonder why I can't focus on the now. Why am I making everything with Declan more complicated? He has been straightforward about the kind of relationships he's interested in—short-term, no strings. What if I could be like that?

I want him. He said he wanted me too.

Even as I think about it, I laugh at myself. I'm getting way ahead of myself. I don't know if I could even pull that off.

Right now, I want to spend time with him. That's simple enough. But am I ballsy enough to ask him out?

Stiffly, I smile at my mother, who's looking at me funny.

"Maybe I will." I snap my computer closed. "Come on. Let's go eat sushi."

Declan

I TAKE BACK EVERYTHING I ever said about seven-year-olds. There is nothing easy about entertaining them.

"These skates are pinching my feet." My half-brother, Stephen, sits on the bleachers next to the rink, tugging at the laces on his skates.

"They're not going to fit perfectly. They're rentals," I explain, trying to hold my patience. I lift one of my feet. "Mine were really expensive, and then I had them heated, so they formed to my feet." I drop my foot. "If you decide to take up hockey like me, we'll get your skates properly fitted as well. For now, you just need something that you can wander around the rink in."

He wrinkles his nose. "Hockey's a stupid sport. You can do it. I'm going to play something cooler."

I grit my teeth but hold my tongue. Since I picked Stephen up, he's been doing everything he can to make this miserable. He complained about traffic, then about being hungry. After a snack, he said that his stomach hurt. We sat and sipped some Sprite for a while, and he watched videos on his phone, pretending I wasn't even there. I was only seconds from demanding he put the thing down, but I refrained. Whatever I said would have been some variety of "I didn't have a phone at your age," destined to make me sound old and uncool.

Then the rink was cold and smelled weird. Now, it's his skates.

"Listen, Stephen. It's pretty clear you don't want to be out."

"What gave that away?" He snorts and rolls his eyes.

Little brat… "But I promised your mother that I'd bring you. So, can you at least stop whining for a few minutes? I actually like to skate."

"Yeah. Wouldn't want to make my mom upset." He wrinkles his nose and gets up, walking on wobbly ankles toward the ice.

I exhale an irritated breath. "Hold on. Let me help you onto the ice." I hustle up behind him, but that only makes him pick up his pace. He steps onto the marble threshold on his blades and promptly loses his balance. Diving forward, I scoop him up before he hits the ground.

"Stop it," he exclaims, wiggling away. "I'm not a baby."

I shuffle him, still struggling, onto the ice. I make sure he's got a good hold on the boards before I let him go. "Sure complain like one," I mutter to myself, but he overhears me.

His face breaks, and for a moment, he looks like he might cry. But as quickly as the sadness is there, it's gone, replaced by anger. "You're an asshole," he says before shuffling along the boards, away from me.

He's not going very fast, so it's easy to catch up. "Stephen, listen, I'm sorry."

He keeps going, ignoring me.

"It's just… you're not making it very easy to be around you today."

"Well, no one thinks I'm easy to be around right now," he fires back, his head tilted up.

"No one?" I ask, easily gliding along next to him. I debate asking him whether he wants to hold on to me but stop myself. He's fired up. I suspect he'll shake off my help.

"No one." He nods solemnly. He casts a glance up, almost loses his balance, and returns his gaze to his feet. "My mom. Dad. No one."

"Why don't you think that Pam and Dad don't want to be around you?" I ask softly.

He lifts a shoulder. "Mom is sad a lot. I even see her cry sometimes. And Dad..." He shakes his head. "He's not home much." His mouth thins. "Since Mom asked for a divorce, he's stayed away a lot."

"He's doing that for your mom, buddy. Not because of you." It's easy for me to say that. I've watched my father go through this before. I have to swallow the urge to bad-mouth him. Stephen doesn't need to hear that from me right now. But seriously, what the fuck? Why can't my father stop being a selfish prick for one minute and see that he's hurting his son?

Railing against him won't help anything, though. Our father is over sixty years old. He's not about to change.

I shift to skate backward next to him, softening my voice. He keeps inching along the side of the rink, but he's watching me now, too. "You know, when Dad broke up with Hillary's mom, he did the same thing. Did you know that?"

Stephen shakes his head.

"Yeah. And after my mom left him..." I swallow. Even though it's been almost fifteen years, I still remember the anger I felt at my father. "He didn't visit me for weeks."

Stephen stops, his eyes on his hands holding on to the side. Finally, he says, "Weren't you... sad?"

I nod before I realize that he's not looking at me. "Yes. I was really sad. And mad."

His tear-filled eyes find mine. But he doesn't cry. "I'm those things too."

I'm not sure if he's going to accept it, but I lean down and pull him into a hug. "I know, bud, I totally get it." He's stiff at first, but then he wraps his arms around my waist, leaning on me. "But that's his problem, not yours. You're a great guy. Our father just needs to grow up."

He does the best he can to glance up at me, but I'm basically holding him up, so it's hard. Even from here, I can see his side-eye. "Declan…"

"What?"

"Dad's old. Not sure if you noticed."

I crack up. He looks at me funny, like he's not sure if he should laugh along with me, but before long, we're both standing there, howling like idiots.

"Let's go." I motion at the rink. "Don't you want to skate?"

He shrugs, apologetic. "I'm not good at this."

I tap my lips as if considering. "Well, come on, then." I hold my hands out to him, and after a moment, he grips my forearms. I shuffle backward, dragging him forward.

"Whoa. Make sure I don't fall," he cries, wobbling along.

"I got you, kid. Don't you worry." He doesn't know it, but I mean it. Our father might have already let him down, but he'll always have me. I'll make sure of it.

Stephen loosens up after that, and we end up having a pretty good time. After he tires of skating, I buy him ice cream from the concession stand. As we sit, we talk about school and what he wants for Christmas. I get him smiling. At the end, I ask if he'd like to hang out with me again before Christmas.

"Sure!" He smiles, his face covered in chocolate ice cream. He glances around as the cone drips onto his fingers. "Do you think we might try skating again? Or maybe you could teach me a little about hockey?"

I narrow my eyes, smothering my grin. "I thought you said that hockey wasn't cool?"

His smile becomes sheepish. "I was just being a jerk. I'm sorry."

I tussle his hair. "No problem. And I'd love to. None of the girls wanted to learn anything about hockey." I consider. "Well actually, Hillary did, but she said she didn't want to hurt her arms, or she wouldn't be able to play piano."

"Hillary is really good at the piano." The kid I picked up earlier wouldn't have willingly given anyone a compliment. I'm taking that as a win.

"She is. We'll get to see her on Christmas. That'll be cool. I bet she'll play all the Christmas carols you want if you promise to be nice."

"I will."

"And cut your mom a break, too, okay? She's doing the best she can." I leave out my father. That guy deserves whatever he gets.

"Okay. I promise."

"Great. All right. Let's get you home."

We clean up our table and dump our trash into the receptacle. As we're heading for the exit, my phone buzzes in my pocket. I shift my skates to my other hand and fish it out.

Ivy: *Salsa*?

I stop, tuck my skates under my arm, and type back, deliberately obtuse: *The condiment?*

Ivy: *No, Mitchell. The dance.* She adds the eye-roll emoji, and I grin.

Me: *Sounds fun.*

Ivy: *They teach lessons at Café Caribe in the Village. Want to meet me there tomorrow night?*

Me: *Are you asking me out, Princess? On a date?* I grin, imagining her flush. I ignore my body's reaction to the mental image.

The typing dots appear and disappear twice. She takes so long to message me back, I wonder if she's going to chicken out. Finally, she sends: *Yes. Do you want to go or not?*

This girl... she's always surprising me. Chuckling, I respond: *You bet. Send me the details. See you tomorrow.*

I slide my phone back into my pocket.

"Why are you smiling?" Stephen asks as we head toward the parking lot.

"Just a girl I know. She makes me laugh."

He wrinkles his nose. "Ew. Girls are gross."

That makes me grin even wider. "Talk to me in ten years, kid."

Ivy

DECLAN IS ALREADY WAITING outside Café Caribe when I arrive on Friday night. I jump out of my Uber, squeeze my arms around myself against the cold, and hurry toward him, my heels clicking on the sidewalk. He glowers at me. "Where's your coat, woman?"

"I didn't want to bring one because I was afraid I'd lose it." He steps between me and the wind and hurries me inside. I'm immediately hit with the heat of the club. "Besides, I was sure it was going to be warm in here."

"You're right." He pushes the sleeves up on his long-sleeved shirt, revealing his tattoos and generally looking like the hottest guy I've ever seen. To keep from drooling over him, I check the place out. The club is extremely festive with brightly colored decorations. It's got good energy. Across the room, the dance floorboards are well-worn, and they make me smile. A lot of fun happens in this room. I can feel it.

I'm glad I did this. When my mother suggested that I take Declan out to a place where we can salsa, I knew it meant I needed to ask Declan to go with me on what's essentially a date. I've never asked anyone out before. But I finally asked myself what I had to lose. After what I went through last year, was I afraid of getting my feelings hurt if he turned me down? It seemed ridiculous from that perspective, so I sent him a text.

Of course, he had to call me on it. *Are you asking me out, Princess?* I grin, remembering. The cocky goofball. I'm sure he didn't expect me to admit it, but if he hasn't figured out that I won't shy away from him anymore yet, he will soon. I already told him I'm attracted to him, and nothing bad happened. A year ago, I wouldn't have taken the chance to make a fool of myself. That seems silly now. I should say what I need to say. What do I have to hide? I'm sick of waiting to take control of my life. Now is the best time.

That's a heady freedom.

As we head toward the dance floor, he takes my hand and leads me through the people milling around by the bar in front. The crowd easily parts for him. He might be the tallest guy in the place, and he's the best looking, by far. Women of all ages watch him go by. I stand taller walking with him.

I've never been to this club before, but a dance friend who specializes in Latin dances said it was the place to be. It's not very crowded for the lessons on Friday night, probably because it's the holiday season and people have other things going on. It works out for Declan and me, though. There's more space on the dance floor for us to move around, and that's a definite perk, considering Declan's over six feet of long limbs and muscle.

I already know how to do the dance. I've never danced it in a performance or competitively, though, so it'll be good to have the refresher. According to my friend, there are lots of people who dance seriously at this club, so we might even find some inspiration.

As I stand next to Declan, excitement streaks through me. I haven't looked forward to dancing like this—for fun, really—in a long time. I'm happy to be here, doing this thing I love with him.

"The dance uses eight counts." Our instructor is a middle-aged woman, but it's obvious she knows what she's talking about. She's got the fluid movements of a seasoned dancer as she steps through the salsa moves. "Let's start with the basic step in place. I'm going to count it out. Starting on your left foot, you'll step forward, then back with your right and return your left to the right. Make sure that you're shifting your weight with every step. After the third step, there's a pause on the fourth beat before we step back with our right foot. Step down on the left on the sixth beat and then return your right foot to the left. Pause on eight."

The group watches her move through the motions a few more times before she turns us loose with a slow salsa beat. As expected, Declan picks it up more quickly than anyone else in the room. If I didn't like him so much, it would annoy me how naturally athletic he is.

After we run through the basic step for a few minutes, our instructor takes her place at the front again. "We'll be doing that basic step in a handful of directions now." She faces away from us again, speaking into her microphone. "First, we'll show it to you from the side." She shows moving to the left, to the established salsa beat and then to the right, keeping with the eight counts. "I'll also show you what we call an 'open break.' It basically means that you'll do the steps in the same direction. So, an open break forward means that you'll move forward with your left foot through the first four counts, and then with your right foot through the second four counts." She demonstrates it again, then allows us to practice on our own, wandering through the group to offer advice.

This process continues. She teaches us the cumbia back and forward, and then she teaches us basic turns. The turning gives Declan the most trouble, but he even picks that up pretty quickly. Before long, she signals to the DJ to cue up some music.

I step in front of Declan. "What do you think?"

He's got the adorable crinkle between his brows that says that he's thinking too hard. He shakes his head, then gives me a mischievous grin. "I'm going to be fine as soon as they get some music going in here."

There's that confidence I'm familiar with. I smile up at him. "Then let's go."

The first song isn't quick, and the instructor requests experienced dancers to stay off the floor. It gives Declan a chance to get his footing. By the time the dance floor opens and the actual music begins, he's got that gleam in his eye as he holds his hand out to me.

"I told you so. You know I'm a natural. Let's show these people what we've got."

Early on, I recognized that I would have a hard time saying no to this man. Now, though, I realize that it's much more dangerous than that. Because I never want to say no to him. When I place my palm against his warm one, I know that whatever happens next will be an adventure.

Maybe I should be afraid, but as always, I'm not. Declan Mitchell is magnetic and electric, and I don't want to deny the chemistry between us. When I'm with him, I feel alive, and after so long just living, I am going to absorb every second of my time with him.

I squeeze his fingers, and this time, I'm the one who winks. "You got it, handsome. I'm with you."

Declan

AS IVY STEPS INTO my arms, I brace for impact.

When she stepped out of her Uber earlier, I knew I was in trouble. She's got on this blue dress... it's not revealing, exactly, except it is. She's totally covered from chin to mid-thigh. It even has long sleeves, but the material is that nearly see-through, thin stuff that leaves nothing to the imagination. Not that my imagination needs any help.

The skirt of the dress is full so that when she dances, it flows around her like a cloud. The color of it, too... it's making her gray eyes almost crystalline. She's gorgeous, but when she calls me handsome and gives me that saucy wink, my dick strains against the fly of my jeans.

God, I fucking want this girl.

The music starts, and we fall into the dance. As always, our bodies find matching rhythms, and she feels like heaven against me. We go through the basic steps, but it's more difficult because this is a faster song. I catch on, though. Dancing isn't that much different from hockey. It requires balance, knowledge of positioning, and the ability to think on the fly.

She adjusts our movements to include a sidestep, and I laugh when she sticks her tongue out at me. Then she hitches up the difficulty. We move around the dance floor, incorporating different variations of the moves. Ivy is a goddess when she dances, but she's different than she was when I first met her. This Ivy is lighter, happier.

I told her I wanted her to relax and have fun, but I never could have predicted how seeing her do that would affect me. In these moments, when she thinks I'm not studying her, when she's caught up in her dance, there's pure happiness in her. I recognize that feeling—the exhilaration of movement, of being perfectly grounded in my body. I live for that, and I chase it, whether by letting loose on the ice, skiing, surfing, or whatever other adrenaline-laced activity I can think of.

I'm drawn to it in her too.

When we misstep, we laugh, and her open glee is addictive. I always want to see her smile and hear her laugh. Before long, we're experimenting with the steps, taking chances. I scoop her up and spin her, letting the sound of her laughter echo in my ears. We stay out on the floor through five songs. At the end of the fifth, we're breathless and glistening in the heated crowd, and my heart pounds loudly in my ears. I haven't felt this free and exhilarated in a long time.

My fingers curl into her hips, and I'm gripping her too hard, I'm sure. I'm not a man who naturally denies my urges. If I don't anchor myself, I'm going to sweep forward, capture her full mouth, and breathe in the pants that are leaving her lips.

Her smile fades as something serious replaces the joy on her face. I need to break the tension, so I lean down and say next to her ear, "Are you thirsty?"

I pull back immediately, though, because the smell of her goes to my head like a double shot of whiskey.

She blinks, confusion and maybe even a little hurt on her face, but she hides it quickly. "Sure." She smiles, her eyes bright. "That sounds great."

"I'll be right back." We aren't far from the bar. I'll be able to see her the entire time, so I'm not technically abandoning her. But I need to take a beat to catch my breath.

I hold up two fingers to the bartender before I catch myself. Ivy hates beer. "One lager, please, and... I don't know, something fruity."

"Fruity?" The bartender eyes me skeptically. "Vague much?"

I wave my hand toward the dance floor. "My girl. She doesn't like beer."

He waves to me and hurries off, and I'm left to watch him pour our drinks while I examine the emotion that hit me when I called Ivy mine. The possessiveness felt too good, and that is definitely bad.

She isn't my girl. I've never had a girl, not like that. I've had countless women in my bed, more than I might even remember. What I just implied, though, is a level of connection that I've never had. It's also something that I shouldn't even want, especially not with Ivy.

She hasn't said as much, but she's not a short-term, casual-bed-partner kind of girl.

I've seen Stephen and Pam twice this week. Pam's heartache and Stephen's anger... those are direct results of what happens when a man thinks he can commit and ends up letting people down. As much as I want to think I'm not like my father, I look like him. Hell, I'm practically his twin. If I want to know what I'll look like at sixty, I only need to see his picture. I've got his easy way with people. I'm a natural extrovert, and I recognize my charisma. Men want to be my friend, and women want to fuck me.

I won't be like my dad, though. I want to be someone people can rely on; someone whose word means something. For a guy who's always struggled to stay focused, it's been a long road to following through. But I'm doing better, and that means I can't start anything with Ivy. We both graduate in a few months. They have not signed me to play in the NHL yet, but I plan to be. And she'll dance professionally somewhere—I'm sure of it. Our futures don't align. I won't start something that we don't intend to finish.

Steady again, I collect our drinks and glance up, searching her out in the crowd. What I see stops me in my tracks. Some guy is holding Ivy's hands, dancing with her. She's smiling, but it's her tentative smile, the one she uses when she's not sure of a situation.

It sours my stomach and sends ice along my spine. In a handful of steps, I'm standing next to her. "Hey, Ivy," I say, my words for her but my hard gaze on her unwanted dance partner. "I got your drink." I hold it out to her, staring down at the guy who is now slowly dropping her hands. Lucky for him, it's only her hands. If he had laid a finger anywhere else, I'm not sure what I would do.

Ivy takes her drink and mumbles something like "thanks," but I don't drop my eye contact with Mr. Handholder. Instead, I raise a brow. "Can I help you with something?" I ask him.

Whatever comes out of his mouth is something like an apology, with some frightened and nonsensical babbling thrown in. When he deems the noise he makes to be enough, he scurries off, practically bowing.

After he's gone, I take a long sip from my beer and meet Ivy's gaze. "What?"

She sighs. "Did you have to scare him? Poor guy looked like he was going to cry."

I drink again, raising a shoulder. I can't work up an apology. "Maybe he shouldn't have been hitting on my date."

"We're not dating." She drops her head, moving to tuck a nonexistent strand behind her ear. She really mustn't be used to her shorter hair yet. She seems to always want to tuck when she's uncomfortable. "We're friends."

"You asked me to come out with you. We're at a club, dancing, together." I swallow a larger gulp of my drink, still trying to soothe my irritation. "That's enough of a date for me."

"You already said you don't date, Declan." She rolls her eyes, but her cheeks are flushed.

I said that, and it's true. But that doesn't mean that I want her dating anyone else, and I certainly don't want to hear about it. I sure as hell don't want anyone hitting on her when we're together on our not-a-date date.

To avoid responding or even addressing that in my own muddled head, I finish my beer. "How's your drink?" I ask.

She opens her mouth like she wants to say something more about this, but then she sighs again. "Delicious." She sees that I'm finished, so she takes a long pull on her straw, downing the rest of her beverage. "Let's dance again."

I can tell she's still irritated, but she hands me her drink glass. I put my empty and her glass on the bar then return to take her hand and lead her back to the dance floor as a song comes to an end. We wait, staring at each other, as the DJ says, "We're going to slow things down now. Find a partner you want to get close to."

I hold her gaze. I can't seem to help myself. Because I want to be close to her more than I want to admit.

What comes on is a blast from my mother's musical library, Sade's "By Your Side." The song's slow and sultry, and the singer's voice is smooth as silk. Around us, couples step together and begin a passionate salsa. I never saw this as a salsa song. It works, though.

I allow my hand to fall to Ivy's hip and tuck her hand in mine. She might be the experienced dancer, but I'm experienced in everything else. She might not understand what's happening between us, but I can see the fire in her eyes, and I feel the answer to it in my stomach. Even though I know it's wrong, that I can't make her promises, I know what this is —it's desire, hot and needy.

She doesn't shy away from me, though. I expect her to. She probably should. She only curls her fingers over the top of my hand. I can feel the erratic beat of her pulse at the base of her wrist, and it fires the burn inside me.

I start us into the dance, and my body curves around hers, close enough to feel the warmth of her as we move in sync. I spread my fingers along the base of her spine, desperate to feel more of her against my palm. Even as I tell myself not to, I bend my head to catch the scent of her—equal parts vanilla, musk, and fresh air, a complex smell for a complex woman.

I follow my heart, pressing my nose against the soft skin under her ear and allowing my lips to reach for her, brushing against the heartbeat feathering there.

Squeezing my eyes closed, I force myself to stop, to retreat even as my entire body screams for a real taste of her. I'd be able to move, too, if she didn't tilt her head the slightest bit. I watch her mouth open, her tongue flitting out to wet her lips. Her eyes are closed, and she's opening, giving me more access to her slender neck. I can't stifle the moan that creeps up my throat as I hold myself steady to keep from dragging my tongue along her soft skin. "Christ, Ivy," I say with a groan, "you're fucking exquisite."

She whimpers, and it's obvious she's also affected because she missteps. It's slight, but it's there.

That gives me pause. Because these reactions aren't supposed to be mine. Nothing about this girl should be for me.

I grip her shoulders and stand upright, stopping us in the middle of the floor. Her eyes open, searching my face, confusion in her expression. "Declan…"

"I'm sorry." I shake my head. "I shouldn't." I'm not lying— I am sorry, but not for the neck kiss. That was delicious. I'm just apologizing for everything else.

"Shouldn't?"

"No. I shouldn't do that. Not with you." A riot of emotions flickers over her face. She spins from me and heads toward the bar.

I follow her, expecting her to stop for a drink. She deserves to be irritated with me. I shouldn't have put her in this position. But instead of stopping at the bar, she continues toward the door, pulling her phone out of some hidden pocket in her dress. When I reach her, she's got the Uber app open.

"Ivy—"

"Stop." She holds her hand up to me. "I'm not listening to this right now." She glares at me and sweeps out the front door.

When I join her, she's already shivering, holding her phone.

I want to fold her in my arms and let her use my body heat, but I don't. It's a fucking herculean physical feat that I keep myself still. Instead, I plead with her. "It's freezing out, Ivy. Let's go back inside."

"You go back inside," she snaps at me.

I can't help but smile. "Very mature."

"You know what's really mature, Declan?" She stands toe to toe with me, her eyes flashing. "A guy telling you he can only be friends with you, and then..." She seems to run out of words for a moment before waving toward the club. "Then acting like that in there."

"Like what?" My question comes out in a whisper.

"Like..." She stares up at the streetlights above us. "Like that."

She blushes, and I take pity on her. "You're right. I shouldn't have done that."

"Why did you do that?" she asks, her voice a whisper. "Why did you kiss me?"

"Because you're beautiful, and I like being with you." I'm no liar. I pride myself on that. That's the truth. "But I shouldn't have. I'm sorry."

"Because I'm not a girl you think you should..." Again, she blows out an exasperated huff. "That you should want to... touch like that?" The way she's struggling with the words to even explain this situation is adorable. It makes me want to tease her more and make her blush deepen. Mostly, it makes me want to drag her against me, to bury my face in her hair, her neck, her skin... to see if I can absorb just an ounce of the sweetness of her.

Instead, I cross my arms over my chest. "Have you ever had a casual relationship, Ivy? I don't mean go out on a few dates, then decide to be friends. I mean, have you ever fucked someone one night and then just given them a head nod when you saw them afterward?" I hate that I'm being so blunt with her, but it's obvious that I need to spell this out for both of us. "Because I have. More times than I can count. In fact, that's how I usually do things. The girls I spend time with are perfectly fine with it too."

"No," she whispers. "I've never had that kind of experience before." I'm sure she wants to hide the consternation on her face, but she can't. Seeing that kind of distaste on her beautiful features almost makes me feel ashamed of myself.

That's why I push forward. "Why haven't you ever had that kind of experience before?" When she doesn't answer, I ask again. "Why haven't you ever had a casual fuck?" A couple who just left the club overhear my question and meet my gaze before looking away. Typical New Yorkers. Pretending privacy where there really is none to be had.

"Stop calling it that," she snaps at me. "It's crude."

"It's not crude, Princess. It's just matter-of-fact."

"If you must know," she squares her shoulders. "I don't let just anyone touch me. Only people I…"

"What?" I whisper.

She meets my eyes, and the honesty there almost brings me to my knees. "Only people I trust."

Something squeezes my chest, making it hard to breathe. I hold her gaze, physically incapable of looking away. Unable to stop myself, I reach for her hand, squeezing it. "Do you trust me, sweet girl?" Her eyes search mine, and suddenly, I don't want to know the answer to that question.

"I do."

The words are lightning through my veins, and I close my eyes, desperate to rein in the need spiraling through me. "You shouldn't." I'm still holding her hand. It's important that she understands this. "You're not casual, and that's all I am. We're graduating. I plan to play in the NHL, and you're going to do whatever talented dancers do. We can't be a long-term thing, even if I could do something like that." My eyes hold hers, pleading. "I can't hurt you. I won't."

She drops her gaze, but her fingers tighten on mine. She closes her eyes for a long moment, and when she looks back up at me, she smiles. "Let's go back inside. I think I could dance some more."

She lets go of my hand, sweeps forward to pull the door open, and goes inside. I'm left standing on the sidewalk, completely unbalanced and wondering what the hell just happened. Even when I run it over in my head, it makes little sense. Ivy peeks her head back out. "You coming?"

With no other actual option, I shrug and follow her back inside.

Ivy

I KEEP THINGS FRIENDLY and relaxed with Declan through the three sessions we use to practice our salsa. I choose another fun song, "Say Hey (I Love You)" by Michael Franti and Spearhead, for our salsa. It's upbeat, and the moves I devise this time are all about a good time. Declan picks it up like a fish to water and dancing it with him is more fun than I ever imagined. We throw in a few dips, and he convinces me he can do a throw. I'm unsure at first, but I don't know why. He executes the toss flawlessly... of course.

Our other dance, the open style one to Francis and the Lights, is solid as well. Now that we've spent weeks together, I can't believe that there was a time when I wasn't comfortable dancing with Declan. It seems impossible now. My body is drawn to his, and I search for his eye contact and his touch as we move. I live for his smile.

I crave him.

After our conversation outside Café Caribe, I realized that if I push Declan too hard, I'm going to ruin the fun I'm having with him, and that is the last thing I want. He's not wrong— I'm not the kind of girl who has ever done short-term or casual. I don't even know if I can. Standing on that sidewalk, I recognized that unless I'm prepared to be the kind of girl he's used to, the sort of girl who is okay with casual, then it's important to keep things light.

Christmas passes quietly amid our practicing. I spend it with my parents. My mom's an only child, and my father's only brother lives in California, so we don't have any family close by. But it's still nice. We eat salmon then curl up on the couch, drink Baileys Irish Cream, and watch *It's a Wonderful Life*. None of us say anything about last year's Christmas when I couldn't keep anything down and fell asleep before dinner.

Two days before New Year's Eve, during our last planned practice session, I enlist my mother to watch our two routines. In the studio in the basement of my parents' house, we perform the two dances I've written.

At the end, my mom blinks at us for a long moment before breaking into a standing ovation. "You're both wonderful," she exclaims, hugging us both. "I could watch you dance together forever."

I could dance with Declan forever, but I don't say that. We're solidly in the friend zone. If that's what he prefers, then I suppose that's the way it'll be. But words like "forever" hit weird when you're firmly friended.

"Thanks, Mrs. Deveraux." Declan offers her the grin that's probably been winning parents over since he was a baby. "I think we have a real chance to win this thing."

"With my Ivy choreographing for you, there's no way you can lose," she says, giving me a side hug. "Are you guys hungry? We can order some food."

"That's okay." Declan grins, heading toward his backpack. "I promised my mom I'd be back for dinner. She's making Italian." I have a sudden desire to meet the woman who makes his face soften like that. But I hold my tongue. He hasn't offered to introduce me or invited me over. We're friends. It's not a big deal.

"Maybe next time, then." My mother grins, nods, and heads back upstairs.

Declan packs up, and I follow him. "I guess I'll see you back at school." His team has a game the weekend after New Year's, so he'll be heading back to campus right after the holiday. I'll go back the following week, a week before classes. We plan to practice some more, but I also promised to help Madame Champion choreograph a dance that will incorporate all the participants in the competition. She thought it would be a fun way to start the second night, to invite all the participants back, even the ones that were eliminated.

I won't see him for a week. I hate how much I already miss him.

He hefts his bookbag onto his shoulders and tucks his hands into the pockets of his sweats. He's already thrown on the hoodie he wore here but discarded it while we worked. With his shaggy hair, tattoos, and those intense brown eyes, he's so beautiful that he makes my chest hurt to look at him.

"You have plans for New Year's Eve?" I ask. I try to keep my tone light. It's not really my business. Maybe he's planning to go out with some girl that is the kind of girl he described, someone to spend a night with and forget. It's not my business. I have no ties to him.

I hate the jealousy that slices me up inside.

"Actually," he starts, his shoulders hunched, "I know it's last minute, but I was wondering if you had plans for New Year's Eve." He shrugs. "I wasn't sure I'd be able to go, but Shea and Linc invited me to Shea's family's New Year's Eve party in town. Turns out I'll be there, so if you'd like to come with me, I'm sure it'll be a good time."

My heartbeat picks up at the chance to spend more time with him, especially on a night like New Year's Eve. But I play it cool. "Are you asking me out on a date?"

"I am," he answers without missing a beat. "What do you think?"

It's nearly impossible to keep the huge smile off my face. "Sounds good. Text me the information, and I'll see you there."

It's still early, so he's taking the subway back to Brooklyn. I force myself not to watch him walk down the block toward the station. Instead, I take the stairs to the kitchen two at a time.

"He's really cute, Ivy." My mom is putting away dishes, towel in hand.

"Who?" My father's an attorney. He came home early for dinner, but he'll probably hole up in his office with briefs after dinner.

"Declan Mitchell." My mom wiggles her eyebrows. "Her dance partner."

I sit on a stool at the kitchen island. "He's a hockey player, Dad. On Chesterboro's team."

"I thought you said that he was a dancer." He pulls his glasses off.

"He's dancing in that competition with me."

"Ah." He nods. "And he's hot?"

"Dad," I chide. "Ew."

"What?" He glances at my mother. "Don't the kids say people are hot anymore?" He appears genuinely confused.

"I think they do, honey. I just think she's grossed out that you said it."

"No one says 'grossed out,' Mom." I grin at her, popping a peanut from the bowl she set out into my mouth.

My parents grumble about words that they used when they were kids in the dark ages or whatever, and I continue smiling, happy to see them so light. They never said it, but I could tell that the stress of me being sick took a toll on them, separately and as a couple. I'll never take small times like this for granted again.

As they banter, I consider Shea's parents' party. If Declan invited me, then he obviously didn't have big plans with anyone else. That makes me irrationally happy. Except he probably wouldn't have an actual date this far in advance, I guess. That doesn't seem like his style.

Still, he asked me. That means he enjoys being with me, right?

People kiss at midnight on New Year's Eve. Does this mean that he wants to kiss me? If he does, that still doesn't mean he will. After everything he said on that sidewalk outside Café Caribe, I bet he'll go in for the hug and leave it at that.

Is that what I want? Absolutely not. I want to kiss Declan Mitchell with every fiber of my being. Would it be the worst thing if I used the opportunity to try it? After all, it's New Year's Eve. Everyone will be kissing.

It would only be a kiss.

I snag another handful of peanuts, wave to my parents, who are still teasing each other, and head up to my room. I need to find something to wear.

Declan

SHEA'S PARENTS KNOW HOW to throw a party. They live in a penthouse, and the views from their place are amazing. While the tourists are all in Times Square, blocks away, this part of the city is relatively quiet. It's still New York City, so it's not silent. But on the upper streets, it's more respectable and less gaudy. I can see Central Park from the balcony, and the snow that fell yesterday makes everything look magical from this high. I know up close it's probably gray and nasty, but I guess that's the beauty of a dozen or so floors.

One of my older sisters had invited all the siblings to her place in Hoboken for dinner earlier, so I picked up Hillary and Stephen, and we made our way across the river. It was nice seeing all four of my siblings in one place. My older sisters are lovely—Gretchen is a day trader, and Melissa is a nurse. Mel brought her daughter, my niece, Reyne, and she s crawling, so that was fun.

The only dim spot in the whole get-together was that my father showed up almost two hours late. We'd already eaten and were having cookies and dessert when he finally got there.

It's always the same excuses. Meetings kept him. He lost track of time. He shows up with gifts and money, so the younger kids forgive him. But Gretchen, Melissa, and I have been down this road with him before. It gets tiring.

He had some gigantic party to go to or something, so he didn't stay long. The entire train ride to drop Hillary and Stephen back at home, I did my best to hide my irritation from my younger siblings. But what the fuck? Stephen's been struggling. Pam said that Dad barely spent any time with him on Christmas, and now this. The whole situation is messed up.

Still, I promised Shea and Linc I would be here, so I came. And Ivy is coming.

Who am I kidding? Ivy's the reason I'm still here, at eleven-thirty, when I really wanted to put in my face and leave at ten o'clock.

"Mitch. Why are you hiding out here?" I haven't heard that voice in months. I smile and turn away from staring out at the city to greet Cord Spellman.

I haven't seen him since he played his first game with the Jersey Jaguars at Madison Square Garden in September. We text a lot, and I keep up with his stats. The guys and I watched one of his games the other night, too. He's killing it out there as a defender, and I couldn't be happier for him.

I extend my hand, which he uses to pull me into a back-slapping hug. "I don't hide, you asshole. I'm thinking."

"Since when did this start?" Cord quips. "The guy I used to play with didn't have time for thinking."

I chuckle. He's not wrong. "How are you?"

"I'm great." His smile says it's the truth. "Congratulations, by the way." I furrow my brows in question, and he slaps me on the shoulder. "On being the captain." He shakes his head. "Personally, I'm surprised you haven't fucked it up yet."

"Still got time," I offer mildly. "Is your better half here?" I glance behind him, looking for Hannah Marshall.

The last time I saw him was the weekend they got back together. I've never seen two people happier to have re-found each other. Cord was always closer to Linc than me, so he didn't confide most details surrounding their breakup and subsequent makeup. That might have also been because I hit on Hannah pretty hard when they first started dating.

Once I figured out how Cord felt about her, I backed off. I mean, I might have kept it up a little just to tease him. It's a lot of fun to mess with him.

"She's inside." He blows air into his hands, rubbing them together. "I just came out here to get my thoughts together." He shakes out his shoulders, stretching his neck from side to side.

"Yeah?" I don't know what that means.

He pulls a black box out of his pants pocket.

"Holy shit, is that what I think it is?"

Cord's face splits into the biggest, brightest smile I've ever seen. "It's not a fucking bomb, if that's what you mean." He opens the lid on the box, revealing a diamond that's as big as a dime.

I throw my arms around him, punching his back. Words spew out of my mouth, mostly "congratulations" and a lot of surprised profanity. "When are you going to do it?"

He shrugs. "I guess right now." He makes it sound anti-climactic.

"Just like that?"

His gaze slides away from me, finding Hannah through the window. She's hugging Shea as Violet watches. She's a pretty girl, and I feel like she's gotten even prettier since I saw her last. She's a singer, and her debut album just dropped. I've been hearing her single on the radio. She's extremely talented.

Cord's face has softened. "Hell yeah. Just like that." He gives me a last pat on the arm and heads for the door to go back inside. That's when I see Ivy.

She's wearing a black dress that fits her perfectly. It's sparkly on the top or something, but I'm too far away to see it exactly. She's wearing big hoop earrings, and her hair is in that mass of gorgeous curls. I'm drawn to her, and I meet her at the door as she moves to join me on the patio. I hold the door open for her.

"You came." It's a stupid thing to say. She said she would, but it's getting late, and I was worrying she wouldn't make it.

"I did. Sorry I'm late. Dinner with my parents ran later than I expected, and then it took a long time to get a car."

"I'm just glad you're here." I mean it. "You look amazing."

She does that blush and nonexistent hair-tuck thing that says she's embarrassed but also pleased. "Thanks. You do too."

I glance down and my dark pants and a button down, pretty much what everyone else is wearing. But I shrug, playing it up. "Of course I do."

She laughs, and I grin. I catch Cord out of the side of my vision, dropping on one knee. Hannah covers her mouth with her hands, and something tugs at my chest.

"Wait a second." Ivy tilts her head. "Is that guy proposing?"

I nod. "That's my friend Cord and his girlfriend, Hannah. They both graduated from Chesterboro last year. They had some rough patches, but they definitely belong together." I watch as Hannah nods repeatedly, then throws her arms around Cord. Everyone around them claps. But Hannah and Cord only have eyes for each other. They kiss.

"That's really sweet."

"Yes." Everyone inside starts hugging and congratulating the couple. I can't help the grin on my face. I'll need to make my way in soon, but right now, I'm happy to be watching it all with Ivy. "They're a great couple. Cord Spellman was the captain of last year's team. That's Hannah Marshall. She's this amazing musical prodigy. You might have heard of her. Goldie?"

I wait for Ivy to process, and her eyes light with recognition, and she nods.

"Yeah, she's great. They're just so young. But people say that when you know, you know."

"You don't think that's true?"

I shrug. "I don't know."

She nudges her shoulder against me. "I mean, don't you want someone to share your life with, eventually? Not right now, but someday?" She stares at the celebrating couple in front of us. "I mean, I do."

I consider. "I guess... I guess I don't know."

"You don't know? How is that something you don't know?"

"My dad..." I exhale. "My dad is Harvey Lowe."

I wait for her to place the name. "Wait, wasn't he in Acid Rain?" Acid Rain was a popular rock band in the late seventies and early eighties, in the age of huge hair and guitar anthems.

I nod. "Yeah."

"That band was huge," she exclaims. "My dad even has one of their albums on vinyl."

"Yeah," I repeat. "My father's been married four times. I have four half-siblings. His most recent wife, Pam, just filed for divorce."

"Four times?" She exclaims. I nod, and she furrows her brow. "That's a lot. But what does that have to do with you?"

For me, it makes perfect sense how those dots connect. I'm surprised I need to spell this out. "My father's made promises to women all his life but hasn't followed through. I don't want to be like that."

"So don't be."

It sounds so simple when she says it like that. Except, I have no experience doing that. No other girl has ever made me consider a relationship. I stare down at her, rocked by that realization. I've never cared that I wasn't the commitment type before, but Ivy makes me wonder if I could be different if I tried.

"It's almost midnight." She makes the observation offhand like she's not sure what she should say, and I cast a questioning look at her. She's still staring inside, so I can't read her expression.

"It is." I motion toward the balcony. "You ever seen Central Park from this high?"

She shakes her head, following me to the railing. There's a standing heat lamp out here, but it's still chilly. She shivers, and I step closer. Someone props the door to the balcony open, and I hear more people arrive. Glancing back, I see Shea hugging her twin brother, Colt. I smile at them, glad I came.

"It's almost quiet up here." She leans on her elbows. "On the street, it's so loud. Always. But up here..." She shakes her head.

I lean back, facing the penthouse, so I can watch her and the people inside at the same time. Servers are passing around flutes of champagne. It really must be close to midnight. "Pretty cool, huh?"

She nods. "Thank you for inviting me tonight." Her voice is entirely too serious, and I glance at her. She's wringing her hands in front of her. "I was hoping we could talk about something."

Inside, the couples have paired off, and people have started counting. *Thirty-five, thirty-four...* "We should go in if you wanted to watch the ball drop," I say offhandedly, but I don't move. Usually, I love to be in a crowd, but today—now—I only want to be right here with her.

She shifts to face me, one arm still on the railing. I fold my hands in front of me, admiring how she looks in the winter moonlight.

Twenty-three, twenty-two...

"I know you said that we can only be friends, that you don't date girls who are long-term girls."

I stand up straighter and turn to face her more fully, searching her face, trying to figure out where this is going.

"I understand that. But I still want to do this."

"Ivy..." I can see the intention in her eyes, and I should move. I should step back, pull away from her—do the right thing. *Ten, nine...*

She inhales a steadying breath and drops her hands to her sides, opening and closing them. She appears to vibrate with anxiety. I couldn't move if I wanted to. *Three, two...*

She rises to her toes, her fingers finding the sides of my face. With the gentlest pressure, she coaxes my head down and presses her lips to mine.

There are fireworks, cheers, and some kind of rushing noise in my ears. She doesn't move, doesn't breathe, only softly brushes her mouth against mine for long, beautiful moments. After what feels like a lifetime, she allows a hint of space between us and rocks back. Her eyes are wide, filled with wonder as she blinks up at me. Next to us, there are still fireworks in the air. I can see them reflected in her beautiful gray eyes.

"Happy New Year, Declan," she whispers, allowing her fingers to fall from my face. "This year, I'm following my heart. That means,"—she exhales an unsteady breath—"it means kissing the boy at midnight."

I close the space between us in one step. I cup the nape of her slender neck in my hand and curve my other around her waist before I cover her mouth with my own again.

Ivy

I'VE THOUGHT ABOUT KISSING Declan for days. I dreamed about it. But nothing—none of my imaginings—is anywhere near reality.

With the confidence I expect, he holds me captive against him. There's nothing tentative about Declan Mitchell. He does everything with single-minded focus—even kissing, apparently.

He's also unpredictable, which is why he takes me completely off guard when he pulls me against him. Couple that with the firm pressure of his mouth, and I gasp against him.

A moment of surprise is all I feel before I'm consumed by him. My quick inhale gives him the opportunity to sweep inside my mouth, and his kiss is everything mine wasn't. I was tentative. I haven't been kissed often, and I certainly have never been the kisser.

But there's nothing uncertain about Declan. With one of his hands in my hair, he tilts my head to gain better access to my mouth and I lean into him, place my hands on his shoulders, and give myself over to this kiss.

And it's magic. If I thought we connected when we danced, then this is a completely different, much more powerful level of communication between our bodies. His mouth isn't bruising, but it's insistent, demanding. I respond to that, kissing him back, my skin on fire and my stomach fluttering like the fireworks next to us.

I cling to him, letting him hold my weight, letting him take this kiss wherever he wants. I don't know what I'm doing, but he obviously does, and it's delicious. The hand he had at the base of my spine has traveled lower, curving around my backside, pulling me closer against him. I can feel the hard length of him press against my stomach, and it makes me burn in a way I've never felt before but recognize.

I want him. Desperately.

"Mitch." Whoever is talking must have already said that a few times because it's got that I'm-repeating-myself edge to it.

Declan raises his head and growls, still holding me like he's afraid to let me go. "Damn it, Reynolds. I'm busy."

Having an audience sends reality crashing down around me. We were kissing. Not just kissing—we were making out. My face is on fire.

Linc offers me an apologetic smile. "I know. I just thought you should know..." He inhales. "Shana is here."

Declan curses under his breath, steadies me, and runs a hand over his face. "Damn." Whoever Shana is, these guys aren't happy about her presence.

"Yeah." He shrugs, tucking his hands into his dress pants. "Shea had to invite her. Just brace yourself."

"Who's Shana?"

"Shea's friend from boarding school." Linc shrugs. "She and Declan are acquainted."

Acquainted... he means in the biblical sense. Declan shrugs, but he doesn't appear ashamed or uncomfortable. Inside, I see Shea hugging a tall girl with long, straight blond hair. That must be her. "She's pretty," I comment. The guys look at me, and I shrug. "What? She is." I fold my arms over my chest. It's chilly out here. Or maybe it's just that after I was so warm against Declan, I'm cold without his heat. "I'm sure she's not the only girl here that you've hooked up with." I glance up at Declan.

He sheepishly rubs the back of his neck.

Jeez... I don't want the details. "Right. So, what's with this particular girl?"

"After our time together..." Declan starts, clearing his throat. "She has tried to rekindle things. She wants to go out, or she invites me to parties when I'm in town. It's been over a year, so it's not as often. I'm always polite, but—"

"And you haven't gone out with her because..."

"I never liked her like that." This time, he holds my eyes, and I can only see honesty there. "She wants something more. If I went out with her, it would lead her on."

Right. He's made it clear that he isn't looking for something long-term.

"So, you think she'll say something tonight, and you don't want to hurt her feelings. Got it." I study the girl he slept with. I'm a dancer, an artist, and I'm pretty good at reading people. She has an open face. "She's Shea's friend?"

"Yeah. Since high school."

I glance up at Linc. "Can I meet her?"

"What?" Declan's eyes are wide with surprise, and Linc's mouth is wide open.

I stare between them. "She's friends with Shea. I'm sure she's nice." I take Declan's hand. "Let's go. Don't be weird. Avoiding her out here is just going to make everything more awkward."

Both guys look like I've lost my mind, but I drag them inside. I haven't had a chance to say hello to Shea since I arrived. I was running late after dinner with my parents, and I wanted to make sure I found Declan in time to kiss him at midnight. I spent all day working up my nerve, and I wasn't going to let anything distract me. Now I make my way to her side. She grins and folds me into a warm hug.

"Hey, Ivy!" She exclaims, stepping back, still holding my hands. "When Declan said he invited you, I was so happy you were going to come."

I'm so glad that I met her, especially before we started back to school. "Thank you for having me." I motion toward the kitchen. "I brought your parents a bottle of champagne."

"Thank you." She squeezes my fingers. "This is my friend Shana." She motions to the girl beside her. "We went to school together."

I hold out my hand, offering her a smile. "Hi. I'm Ivy."

Shana gives me a tentative smile, but her eyes find Declan behind me. "Hi. It's nice to meet you." She nods to Declan with another uncertain smile. "Hey, Declan."

He leans forward and hugs her. "Hey."

"Does anyone need a drink?" I ask. I motion to Shana's empty hands. "It looks like you just got here and have nothing yet."

"You're right." She grins, seeming to rally now that she's said hello to Declan. "I'll come with you?"

"Great." I turn to Shea. "In the kitchen?"

"Yeah, unless you want champagne. That's being butlered."

"I think I'll see what we have." I loop my hand through Shana's arm. "Let's go." We weave through the crowd until we end up in the kitchen next to a table full of alcohol. I study it doubtfully. "Do you know how to make anything out of this stuff?"

She takes me in and seems to decide something. Her face splits into a confident grin. "Oh, honey. I've got you." What comes next is a whirlwind lesson on how to make a chocolate martini. As she mixes, Shana's eyes find Declan again. "So, you and Declan, huh?"

He stands with the couple that just got engaged. I don't know them, but he obviously does. He's smacking the guy on the back and twirling the girl around. I smile at him. "No. Not really."

"Really?" She's skeptical.

I wish it wasn't true, but I'm not a liar. "I mean, he's not exactly with anyone ever, is he?"

"No." She considers. "I suppose not." She hands me a martini glass and holds hers up for a clink. "He is a lot of fun, though, isn't he?" I'm sure she doesn't intend the words to sound so wistful, but they do.

I don't know that as well as she does. I tap my glass with hers and take a sip, using that as an excuse not to answer.

Having her here puts the kiss we just shared into perspective. More than a few women have had a taste of Declan Mitchell. When I came tonight, I told myself I knew exactly what I was getting into and that it would be just a kiss. But a small part of me wanted the fairy tale. That silly part wanted him to kiss me and find whatever was missing in his life or have some sort of crystallizing moment.

I snort laugh in my drink. That's ridiculous. But he makes me happy when I'm with him. There are worse reasons to want to spend time with someone. I definitely don't regret that kiss. It was everything I've been missing in kissing. If that's what it's supposed to feel like, the other few guys I've kissed haven't been doing it right. I've obviously been kissing the wrong guys.

"Nice place, huh?" Shana asks.

I nod. Shea's parents' home is beautiful. Even I know who Rory Carmichael is. He's a wealthy real estate developer, and it makes sense that this place in the middle of one of the most expensive neighborhoods in New York would belong to someone like him.

Behind us, guests are going upstairs. "Have you ever been here before?"

Shana shrugs. "Sure. Shea and I have known each other forever."

"Would you show me around? This place is stunning."

She loops her arm through mine, balancing her martini glass with the other hand. "Absolutely. I bet they're dancing upstairs."

"Now, you're speaking my language."

Declan

I LOSE IVY. AFTER she goes to the kitchen to make a drink with Shana, I stop and congratulate Cord and Hannah. They both look almost disgustingly besotted. If they weren't such great people, it might be sickening to watch the sweetness. But all I feel is excitement for them.

After that, I get caught in a handful of conversations. I talk with Shea's father, who's one of the most interesting people I've ever met. He owns a multi-billion-dollar real estate company. Then I get waylaid by two of Shea's brother's teammates. They're all members of the Philadelphia Tyrants NHL team, and we chat about how their season is going. After that, I say hello to a couple of Linc's friends and a few people I've met from Shea's boarding school. During the summer and holidays, they have invited me to a handful of events with both of them, so I know a lot of the people here. But Ivy doesn't, so I'm surprised that I don't see her anywhere. At one o'clock, I give up casually looking for her and search her with manhunt-style focus.

Upstairs, a space has been cleared, and there's a deejay playing music. Ivy is in the middle of the dance floor. I grin. I don't know why I bothered to look anywhere else for her.

Across the room, Shana is talking with two of Colt's teammates. She waves but goes back to chatting without offering me another glance, so I go back to watching Ivy. There are a bunch of people dancing, but she isn't with any of them. That explains Ivy better than anything else. Even in a room full of others, she stands out—or apart. Both, somehow.

I move through the crowd toward her as if I can't stay away.

We haven't talked about our kiss. That surprises me. She could have found me after getting her drink with Shana. But she didn't, and I don't know why. She doesn't strike me as a girl who kisses people casually. In fact, everything about the way she placed her lips on mine screamed inexperience and innocence. It also fired me up more than any kiss in recent memory. That's why, against every warning bell going off in my brain, I clutched her. The entire experience was erotic and innocent and absolutely perfect. Even thinking about it now, I want to kiss her again.

Except one mistake is forgivable, and two are not. That's what that kiss was, too—a mistake. I shouldn't have touched her at all. She might be innocent, but I'm not. I know what I'm doing, and I most certainly shouldn't be doing it with her.

I can't seem to stay away from her, though. More importantly, why won't she let me? I don't know how many other ways I can tell her I'm not good for her. I've tried to warn her off.

But there she is, dancing as if unaffected. I'm the one making too much out of the kiss. I'm the one who wants to know why we aren't talking about it and ask a bunch of questions about what it means. Some playboy I am. I snort, laughing at myself.

Her eyes are closed, and her head is back as if she's totally in the moment and there is nothing on her mind except the music.

I need to get a grip. Maybe it's as easy as this. If she isn't going to look too deeply into it, I shouldn't either. There's no reason for me to be standing here, playing archaeologist with my emotions.

"The Twist" comes on. Not the music that we're used to. It's more wedding reception than frat party, but Ivy doesn't care. She transitions right into the dance, not missing a beat.

To avoid whatever chaos is in my head, I join her. Even before I touch her, she opens her eyes as if she senses me. That thought is unsettling, but I push it aside. The smile on her face is the stuff of men's dreams, and it tightens my throat. All I can squeeze out is "Hi."

"Hey," she says, her eyes soft on me. "Watch out. I'm extremely good at this dance." She throws her head back, hamming it up, and I can't help but grin along with her. I break out dancing, twisting my ass along with her like a fool. She giggles, and I immediately feel lighter and freer. That's what this girl's laugh does—it makes everything better.

Everything inside me, every instinct that I possess, has leaned toward that goal—to see Ivy smile.

I look away from her, wrestling with that realization. Nothing in my experience with the opposite sex has ever felt like that. I like women. I like their bodies and the way they think. That's completely different from this. This... it's as if I want to wrap her happiness around me like a blanket.

To distract myself, I lean forward and ask, "How is everything with Shana?" So what if I allow myself to bask in her vanilla musky scent?

She shrugs, still dancing. "Fine. She's really nice."

She says nothing else, so I wrinkle my brows, trying to figure it out. "You're taking this much differently than I expected you to."

"How exactly was I supposed to take it?"

I don't have an answer that doesn't make me sound like a complete asshole. Did I want her to be jealous? No… or yes? I don't know, so I deflect. "Catfight?"

She laughs. "I'm literally the most useless person in a fight." She makes a muscle with her arm, rolling her eyes, but she's in great shape, so it doesn't look as pathetic as she probably thinks it does. "No, she made me a martini, and we girl talked."

Again, she says nothing more, and that's not enough information. "About me?"

"You wish." The song ends, and "Celebration" comes on. "Fine, she asked me about you."

I scowl at her. "What did she say?" This is like pulling teeth.

"You are incredibly nosy." She rolls her eyes. "We both agree that you're great. A lot of fun to be with." She smiles, squeezes my arm, and continues dancing like that isn't the biggest non-answer she's ever given.

I should be happy that she's letting this go. No one wants their old hookups talking smack about them. The way Shana describes me is almost complimentary compared to what some girls might say. But how Ivy accepts this description of me— some guy who's fun to be with—well, it's the most unsatisfying explanation I've ever heard.

I don't only want to be fun. Not to her. Whatever's happening between us is more than that. It shouldn't be because I'm no good for a girl like her, but I want it to be.

I motion toward the bar. "Are you thirsty?" I need a drink right now more than I've needed a drink in a long time.

"Sure. I can drink."

I snag a beer out of the mini-fridge and see a pitcher of some mixed drink in there, which I pull out and show to Ivy.

"Looks good to me," she says, so I pour her a glass.

We take a drink, watching everyone else dancing and having fun. Well, she watches the dancing. I watch her. Finally, I say, "When will you be back on campus?"

I need to be back in a couple of days. We have two practices scheduled, and then we start right back up with our game schedule on Friday night. Playing a winter sport means spending the last two weeks of winter break on campus.

"Not for another week." She sets her drink down on the bar. "I'm supposed to meet with Madame Champion when I get back. She wants me to choreograph a dance number for all the participants that we'll do at the beginning of the second night of competition."

"She picked you?"

She nods, obviously pleased by that.

"You're going to do great."

"Thanks." She takes another sip.

Into the silence, I blurt out, "Come to my hockey game on Friday." I don't realize I'm going to say the words until they're out, but I'm not sorry for bringing it up. "It's in Connecticut, but that's only an hour train ride from here."

"You want me to come to Connecticut on Friday? To watch you?" She looks as stunned as I feel. But now that I've offered, it's the perfect idea. Otherwise, I won't see her for over a week. No more private dance sessions or salsa or childish competitive bantering. No Ivy for a week is like a physical pain in my stomach.

"Yes. If you're not busy and you want to." She blinks up at me, and I'm sure she's going to turn me down. It's a lot to ask someone who you insist is only a friend.

But she smiles. "I would love to."

I studiously ignore how relieved I am that she agreed. I toast her with my beer bottle.

I'll see her again soon. I focus on that.

Ivy

SHEA'S ALSO GOING TO the game in Connecticut on Friday, so instead of taking the train, she drives us there. We get a room in the same hotel that the guys are staying in that night, and after check-in, we head straight for the arena.

The game isn't even a real contest. Our team dominates. There's never a point where we lose control of the situation or fall behind in scoring. More importantly, Declan is at his best. There are moments when I think he might go rogue and do something unpredictable or impulsive, but he remains focused the entire time. It's a decisive win, and everyone knows it.

We don't get a chance to see the guys before they head back to the hotel, so we follow the bus. The guys file out, and we get swept up into the celebration as the team funnels into the lobby and up the stairs. They all seem to room on the same floor, so there's a party mentality about it here. They propped all the doors open, and people are streaming between the rooms.

Scratch that—a couple of doors are closed, and there are "Do Not Disturb" signs hanging from the knobs. I guess girlfriends, other than Shea, made the trip for the game.

The guys don't have another game the next night, so they bust out some cases of beer, and the coach remains conspicuously missing.

After about an hour, Shea pulls me aside. "I have a huge favor to ask." She smiles sheepishly. "Would it be okay if maybe you stay away from our room for a little while?" Her face flushes. "Not even an hour, just for a bit." She shrugs. "Since we've been home for the holiday, I haven't had much time alone with Linc, and... well..."

I smile. "I completely understand." Around us, the party's still in full swing. "This is still crazy. I'm sure I can keep myself busy here for a while. Have fun."

She grins and escapes to the stairwell, waving as she disappears. I wave back, happy to see my friend so carefree.

There's only beer, so I find a bottle of water and just hang out with Declan and his roommates in the hallway. It was Linc's first game back and apparently it requires a bit of analysis. They all think he played great. The talk turns to how this proves they could make a real run for the playoffs again this year. That prospect sends a crackle of excitement through the group, but they pretend it doesn't.

It's late, and I'm tired, so I head to Linc and Declan's room. The door is open, so I go in and plop down on the bed to wait an appropriate amount of time for Shea to hook up. Problem is, I don't know what that is, so I end up lying down and messing around on my phone. I figure Linc will return when the coast is clear.

I must have fallen asleep, though, because I wake up to a dip in the mattress next to me. I shoot up to sit, disoriented, and find Declan with his finger to his lips, shushing me. "It's just me."

I glance around, struggling to get my bearings. "What time is it?"

"Late." He studies me with lidded eyes. "What are you doing here?"

"Shea wanted the room for a booty call with Linc." I tuck my knees up under my chin, still groggy. "I was waiting until he came back before I went up. I didn't want to interrupt anything."

"I was wondering where he went. Should have known." He clears his throat. His face is closed, not open and mischievous like I'm used to, his eyes steady on me. This Declan is more intense. I can't read him.

"What?" I wipe at the sides of my mouth. "Was I drooling?"

"No, Ivy. You weren't." He continues to stare at me, his brown eyes fixed on my face. "Why haven't we talked about it?"

His voice is husky, and it sets off shivers along my skin. "About what?" I whisper.

"The kiss. Why haven't we talked about it?"

Oh... the New Year's Eve kiss. I tuck my chin, but I can't look away from his gaze. "I didn't know you wanted to talk about it." I've thought about it. In fact, I've relived it in my head at least a hundred times. More, probably.

"I'm talking about it now." He shifts closer, squeezing my ankle.

"What do you want to talk about?" I hug my knees to my chest.

"Why?"

"Why what?"

"Why did you kiss me?"

"It was New Year's Eve, Declan." It's the coward's answer, but I'm not as strong here, drowning in the intensity of his gaze, as I wish I was. "Everyone kisses at midnight on New Year's Eve." That might be the cop-out explanation, but my next question takes a lot more nerve. "Why did you kiss me?"

"Because I needed to."

"You did?"

He nods. "You shouldn't have kissed me, though."

"You keep saying that." I scoot off the bed, but I'm careful to dismount on the side that he's not on. I stand with my hands on my hips, glaring at him. "Stop telling me what I should or shouldn't want to do." I wave him over. "No one gets to be the keeper of what I want. If I want to kiss the hot guy, why can't I do that?" I stop, my eyes widening. "I mean… if he wants to kiss me, too. Oh God. Unless you didn't really want to kiss me." He said he needed to kiss me, not that he wanted to. What does that even mean? "Was your kiss… a pity kiss?"

Maybe he felt bad for me. I'm not a good kisser. Not because I'm not willing, but I just don't know what I'm doing yet. I'm aware I need more practice. I need more practice in every aspect of making out.

"Fuck no." He looks genuinely horrified. "That's not what I said."

"So, you wanted to kiss me?" I'm getting irritated. "I'm not good at reading all these signals, Declan. What are you trying to say here?"

"I'm saying that I wanted to kiss you. Fuck, Ivy, I always want to kiss you. But you shouldn't want to kiss me."

"Why not?" I say, exasperated.

He lowers his brows. "You're sweet and fine, and you're too good for some stupid casual thing with me."

"Well,"—I cross my hands over my chest—"you don't get to tell me that. And if you wanted to kiss me, too, then I don't see what the problem is."

He buries his hands in his hair. "The problem is that I still want to kiss you, Ivy," he growls. "I want to kiss you and hold you. Christ, I find you here, in my fucking bed, and do you know what kind of inappropriate images that puts in my head?" He paces on his side of the bed. "You're probably all warm, and I know already how soft your skin is. Like silk. I also know how you fit against my body because I've danced with you dozens of times." He drags his hair through his fingers, making it stand up straight. It shouldn't look so good, but there's literally nothing I can imagine that Declan could do that would make him unattractive to me.

"Don't even get me started on the night I held you last year. I keep revisiting that. Not because we did anything, but now I know you." His words are gravel. "I know your smile, the way you laugh. I know the way you say what you're thinking. But what you're really thinking, not just the bullshit fake things that people say to make conversation. And I know that when you dance with me, your face comes alive, and I wonder if you look like that when you come." He shakes his head. "And God, I want to know."

My entire body is on fire, and it's not only because no one has ever said anything like that to me before—it's because it's Declan. I close my eyes on the vision of me orgasming while he watches, my breath hitching.

"Fuck…" The word is a groan, and it makes me whimper. "You need to leave before this gets out of hand." He moves toward the door, his back toward me. "I'm sure that Linc and

Shea are done. It's been two hours. I'll even walk you up there and drag his ass out so you can sleep."

"I'm a virgin," I blurt out. Immediately, I cover my mouth, but that's never been an effective strategy to call back words.

He stills completely. He's facing away, having headed for the door. Long seconds pass, and neither of us says anything, but the time feels like it's warped, infinitely longer than real time could possibly be. The words linger in the air between us, and something becomes clear to me. "I'm not embarrassed."

He slowly turns to look at me, but I can't read his face. It doesn't matter, though, whatever he's feeling.

What matters to me right now is me—how I'm feeling and what I want and making sure that I say what I need to say. "Before I got sick, I was busy. All I cared about was dancing and my goals and my dreams. I didn't have time for dating and relationships. I assumed I'd get to it later. Maybe that's true. Maybe I've just met no one I wanted that close to me. But you are so much more than that."

He shakes his head, but I put up a hand to stop him. "Not because you're a great kisser, though you are a great kisser." I exhale a shaky breath. "But I like you. I like to be with you, and I always want to be with you, whether we're walking to the deli or dancing at a salsa club. You make me... happy. Free." I cover my chest. "Alive."

"Ivy, Jesus..."

I keep going because I'm not done. "My Hodgkin's lymphoma was stage three. I went through a lot of stuff, but I lived. There were days—this doesn't make me proud—but there were days I wasn't sure I would. Sometimes, I felt so miserable and so sick, I wondered if I should. But what I learned, if nothing else, is that living for the future is stupid.

I'm here right now." I drop my brows. "If I want to kiss you, and you want to kiss me, then that's what I want. So don't tell me, Declan Mitchell, that I should or shouldn't want something. Never again will I deny a feeling or an emotion. At least not one like this." I glare at him. "You taught me that."

I inhale a steadying breath before I continue. "Why did I kiss you? Because I wanted to. I still want to kiss you. A lot. And I want to do other things as well, if you do too. I might not know what I'm doing, but I want to try. Not because I'm looking for a long-term thing. I'm not. I'm alive now. So, if you also want those things as well, then you let me know."

I raise my head and prepare to leave. It would have been a respectable exit. I'm a performer—entrances and exits are important to me. But as I reach the door, he grabs my hand.

"Hey, Ivy," he says, as he spins me around to face him. I glance up, meeting his eyes. Brown eyes get a bad reputation. Sure, they're the majority, but his aren't normal brown eyes. Sometimes they're lighter, like caramel. Sometimes they're dark, like the richest coffee. Right now, they're the color of rich chocolate, and I can't look away.

"Yes?" The word is breathy, needy. It negates all the girl-power strength in my speech a minute ago.

"I'm going to kiss you again. Right now." He runs his hands up my arms, and I lean into him.

"God, yes."

Declan

A VIRGIN. IT'S SHOCKING.

There's nothing wrong with virginity. I respect anyone's desires regarding their body and their right to do with it as they please. Sexual preferences, sexual partners… any sexual situation. If the partners are consenting and everyone's legal, it's fair game in my book. That means that if people want to be sexually active or not, that's their business. No judgment from me.

From the beginning, I assumed Ivy was inexperienced. It was the main reason I told myself to steer clear, to keep my distance. She's so sensual, though, so responsive. She loves movement, and she lives in her body so fully. I expected that she would have experimented with that.

What surprises me is my response to her declaration. Every inch of me wants to have her, to claim her as mine. I never, not in one million years, would have expected that I was that kind of guy—a possessive guy. But this is Ivy. She doesn't trust people lightly, and she doesn't want just anyone to touch her.

She wants me. She chooses me. Not because of the way I look. Not because I'm a hockey player or have any particular reputation. Some girls have slept with me just because I'm a player, and they want to brag that they've been in my bed. It's never really bothered me. If it's fun, if we're both enjoying ourselves, I don't see any harm.

But this... she doesn't want any of that from me. She only wants me. This sweet, feisty, brave girl wants me.

I fold her against me, and she's shaking. I brush a curl off her forehead and hush her. Then I capture her mouth with mine.

Like the last time, she tastes sweet and warm like vanilla, molasses, and spice. It's completely intoxicating. I deepen my angle so I can get more of her, sipping at her mouth. She opens for me, meeting my kiss. She's eager, unembarrassed. There's nothing coy, just honest desire in her.

I break the kiss and stare down at her face. There's trust there. Whatever happens next, I need it to be something that's good for her. I also know that I need to slow down. I've never been with a virgin, not even when I was a virgin myself. I don't trust myself with her first time—not now, maybe never. But there are lots of things that we can do that will be good for her without me having to hurt her.

I lean over, sweep her up in my arms, then deposit her in the middle of my bed as gently as I can. I follow her down, curling her against me. I lie there, listening to my own heartbeat in my ears as I hold her.

"Declan?" she whispers, and she's practically vibrating.

I wrack my brain, searching for something to ease the tension. "Yeah?"

"Are we just going to snuggle again? Because I've got myself all nervous, so if we're only going to snuggle, I might die of unrealized anticipation." She says it like a confession, and I snort a laugh.

"Is that a legitimate cause of death?" I tickle her.

She giggles, and it has the desired effect. Now, she's smiling up at me, and I drag a finger along her cheek.

"I stand by that night of snuggles."

"Why did we only snuggle that night?" The lighting in hotel rooms is weird. Sometimes it's too bright. Other times, it's shadowy and dark. But right now, the light from across the room casts a soft glow on Ivy's face, and her gray eyes are big.

"Don't hate on snuggling." But I answer her seriously. "That night, Linc got hurt. Concussion. He lost consciousness on the ice. He's back now and fine. But I remember thinking that it could have been me. That could have been me laid out on the ice, my career in jeopardy. I didn't understand why it was him, not me. I take more risks." I run my fingers over her hair. "You seemed to understand that. When I held you, it was okay that I was..."

"Scared?" she offers.

I nod. I don't even think I realized that was what it was that night. But I had been terrified at how quickly things can change.

"That next day, I drove home. That Monday, I started chemo." She winds her fingers in mine. "I was scared too."

I drop my mouth to hers. This time, our kiss is different. It's deeper, more meaningful. I want to drown in her, to stay there forever. I pull her up so that we're sitting, facing each other. I reach for the hem of her sweater.

She draws away, meeting my eyes again.

I wait, holding her eyes. "If you don't want to go any further ever, you say so."

She nods.

"Do you want to stop?"

She shakes her head.

I chuckle. "You're going to need to use more words."

"Don't stop." She scoots back so she can pull the sweater over her head.

Her bra is nude lace, and I can see the extent of the tattoo along her collar. I raise my hand, allowing my finger to feather along the lines of it. "This covers the scar you had, doesn't it?"

"My biopsy. This lymph node…" She traces the spot, her eyes far away. "Not my only scar." Her fingers flutter to the other side of her chest, to a circle-shaped mark. I let my eyes follow her hand. "Port. For chemotherapy."

I lean my head down and kiss this new scar, allowing my tongue to lick her skin in a long, slow lap. When I raise my eyes to hers, I say, "I kissed the biopsy scar already, the night we first met. Do you remember?"

She nods.

"Are there more?"

She drops her eyes from me.

I catch her chin with my finger. "No, don't look away. I think you're gorgeous." I wink at her. "But I can't miss any."

She leans up and turns, revealing a minuscule tattoo of a lion on her hip. "It was here. My bone marrow biopsy."

Jesus Christ… the things this girl went through… it makes my heart ache. "May I?" My voice is barely recognizable as I motion to the lion.

"Declan…"

"Yes or no, Princess." We've come too far for her to shy away now. "Yes or no."

"Yes," she says, glaring up at me. "You brat. Yes."

Quickly as I can, I snag her legs and tug her, so she falls onto her back with a squeal. "I'd like to taste that lion, pretty girl."

She turns, offering me her flank with a giggle. But her laughter fades as I drop my mouth to her skin, and she goes completely still as she watches me over her shoulder. I hold her eyes as I rain kisses along the tattoo, then keep going. There's nothing in the world that tastes as good as her skin on my tongue and lips. She leans forward on her elbow, allowing me more access to her back, and I can't keep my touch to just my mouth.

I trail my fingers along her skin as I gently nip at the sensitive spot under her arm. "Ivy?"

Her answer is a distracted hum.

"Your bra's pretty, but it'll look better on the ground."

She's a dancer, and that's probably how she's got the front clasp unsnapped and the string of lace flying across the room in a split second. Either that or she's a contortionist. Whatever it is, she reaches for me, and I get my first full view of her breasts, and they stop me cold.

I adore the female form, but the way she's shaped is more appealing to me than any other shape I've ever seen. Her breasts are small, but the tips are tight, like stars, and they're the color of strawberries.

With a finger, I trace the outline of one, and she gasps. The sound is achy, and it urges me forward. I suck that perfect strawberry tip into my mouth. She comes off the bed, arching into me, and I murmur against her in approval. I rain attention on her breasts, her belly, sliding my hands along her, desperate to touch every part of her I can reach.

At the waistband of her leggings, I glance up her body and meet her gaze. What I see on her face steals my breath. If Ivy's beautiful on a regular day, in my bed, with sex in her eyes, she's the hottest thing I've ever seen.

I wrestle down the sharp lust that rockets through me. "Ivy?"

"Yeah?"

I swallow hard. "Can I please take your pants off and lick you?" Her lips part on a soft inhale, and my fingers grip the fabric between me and what I want. She nods, but that's not going to be good enough. Not for first times. "Princess, I need a yes or some active participation."

"Right." She scoots up. "Yes. Actively yes." She lifts her hips, pulls her leggings down along with whatever underwear she's wearing. She slides it all down her legs with in that spandex. She struggles with the elastic at her ankles, and I cover her hands with mine.

"I can take it from here, baby."

She stills, uncertainty on her face, so I stop too. "What's up?"

"I don't know..."

I tense, afraid of where this is going, but ready to do whatever she needs. "What?"

"I don't know how this is going to feel." Color erupts on her face and across her collarbone. "I mean, I've imagined it before, but well... is it weird?"

Relief courses through me. That's not a stop, it's a pause to process. *Thank God.* I can work with that. "For you? Not if I'm doing it right." She shifts her feet, tugging at the ankles of her pants again, so I help her with them until the damn straightjacket-like things are on the ground. "For me, this is going to be amazing."

"How do you know that?"

From any other girl, I might think that question is coy or seductive. But Ivy's serious. I consider the question with the same gravity she asked it. "Because if you taste as good there,"—I touch her hip—"as you do everywhere else, it'll be heaven." I lean forward to kiss her, dragging her lower lip between my teeth. "What I expect is a combination of the softness of your mouth,"—I drop my head to run my tongue along the side of her neck—"and the delicious musky vanilla smell of you." She leans back on her elbows as I drag my mouth down her body. I want to breathe her in. "But what I'm really looking forward to is the slickness. Are you wet for me, pretty girl? That's what I can't wait to find out. My guess is that you are, and just thinking about it has me hard."

Her breath comes in soft pants. Imagine that… my Ivy likes some mild dirty talk. I continue. "Do you know why I think you're hot and wet and ready for me? Because your nipples are so tight, they might even hurt." I drop my head again, keeping my lips soft as I take one hard tip in my mouth and then the other, rolling each one on my tongue. Her eyes have fallen closed, and I use the break in contact to drink in the sight of her. "Do you think you're wet for me?"

Her head drops back, and she gives herself over to whatever feelings are coursing through her. I lick my lips because this is exactly where I want her to be. Relaxed, warm, and soft underneath me.

No one has ever touched her like this. I tamp down on the roar of possessiveness that washes over me. I don't have a right to that because I have no intention of being her first. If she's waited this long, she's waited for her first time to matter, not to be with some playboy who only knows casual. I want that for her, too.

That doesn't mean I can't give her pleasure. Hell, I'm dying to worship her body. I slide down until I'm positioned between her legs, my eyes on the center of her. She's completely bare, and I swear, I almost come in my pants. I slide my fingers along the inside of her thighs, allowing her to adjust to my touch here.

"I'm going to lick you now, Ivy," I whisper against her. "I'm going to lick you and suck you and touch you. Is that all right with you?" I wait. God, they're the longest moments of my life, but I wait. She says nothing, so I glance up at her. "Ivy?"

"Please, Declan... just, please..."

I press her legs farther apart. "Fuck, yeah." I breathe against the center of her as I lean forward and drag my tongue across her core, and I'm lost.

Ivy

THE ONLY THOUGHT THAT crosses my mind is that whatever Declan is doing with his mouth shouldn't be legal. After that, I can't concentrate on anything else.

I've touched myself before, but this is completely different. I'm lost in the feeling of his mouth against me. My fingers dig into the sheets, holding me still because I don't want to do anything that interferes with what he's doing. I'm not sure exactly where he's taking me, but he seems to know. Every change in pressure, every slight movement of his mouth or hands, it all pushes me forward, building me up and up until the world is lights and stars. My whole body explodes in my orgasm, sending me soaring. I call his name along with a whole lot more sounds I don't recognize ever making before.

He continues until I calm, slowing with the tension in my body until I'm nothing but fluid limbs and happy sighs. Then he crawls up my body and gathers me against him, curling me in.

I can only breathe, my brain incapable of distinct thoughts, only feelings and sounds. When I finally put together something to say, it's not brilliant. "Wow."

He chuckles. "What a nice compliment."

I laugh, but the movement of that presses my backside against the hard length of him. He wants me, I can feel that, except he doesn't seem in any hurry to do anything about it. I'm ready for him. I search for something to say, but I don't know how to act in these situations, so I only feel awkward. "What are you thinking?" I ask.

"What do you mean?"

"I mean..." I rotate to face him. "Why aren't we... you know..." Jesus, is he going to make me spell this out? "Why aren't we having sex?"

He stiffens in my arms. He sighs, staring over my head. "Ivy..."

I don't like the sound of that. "What?"

"You don't want to have your first time with me." I open my mouth to argue, but he stops me. "Let me rephrase. I don't want you to have your first time with me."

Embarrassment burns through me, and again, I'm infinitely aware that I'm completely naked. "What? But why?"

He runs his hands along my back. "I told you. I'm not a long-term someone."

"Maybe I don't want a long-term someone."

He gives me a disbelieving smirk.

"What? You don't know what I want."

"You waited this long, Ivy." He kisses my forehead. "Don't pretend you don't want what you want."

I do eventually want a long-term someone. But at this moment, I only want what's in front of me. I refuse to be somewhere else, far away. This man, with his gentle touch and his tender eyes... I want him. I don't want him to stop whatever he's doing. "Right now, I want to see you."

"Of course you do," he says, winking at me, and I laugh. As always, he knows how to defuse seriousness. But I'm not joking. I do want to see him. I reach for his shirt.

Between the two of us, we hustle him out of his clothes in record time. He needs to get off the bed to kick out of his sweatpants, though, and when he's naked, he poses like a bodybuilder. "What do you think?"

His tattoos run along his arms and chest. I remember the nipple ring from last year. His body is in top shape, but I knew that. Declan's one of the most hands-on people I've ever met. He loves to touch and be touched. Between his physical personality and dancing with him all the time, I'm well aware of how he's shaped. I answer him honestly. "You're perfect."

His grin is teasing as he nods. "Right?"

I shake my head at him, smiling. "I've never met someone as confident as you."

"It's not really confidence, exactly." When I cock my head in question, he holds my eyes as he sits next to me, covering my hand on the bed. His expression becomes serious. "In middle school, I was the kid who couldn't focus, who was impulsive. I still struggle with that. I talked too much and always out of hand. My brain was all over the place, usually five steps ahead or off on a tangent. I got diagnosed with ADHD, but the medicines only made me anxious or caused me to hallucinate. I spoke with cognitive behavior specialists, and I learned strategies to manage some things that caused me trouble in school. Breathing techniques. Routines. Lists." He shrugs. "Some worked, some didn't. What works best for me is sports. Hockey taught me about working on a team and helped calm my brain.

"I definitely wasn't the popular kid. Girls didn't notice me then. I was tall and gawky. Not scrawny, but definitely not anything to look at. I needed braces, and my pre-teen skin?" He shivers. "Yikes. Plus, I was active, struggled to sit still and stay on task, and my shit was a mess all the time. I couldn't find things, lost everything. If left to my own devices, my clothes barely matched, and I didn't care. My mother used to laugh at me because my socks were never the same color. My head was in the clouds and on other things. Why do you think I mostly wear gray and black now?"

"Because you look hot in it?"

"Please. It's because it all goes together. Much easier." He snorts. "When girls started to think I was good-looking, I thought it was a joke. I was the kid teachers reprimanded in class, the one they told to sit down, to pay attention. That kid irritates people. I knew it was annoying, but I couldn't help myself." He waves over himself. "Then suddenly, I looked like this, and girls didn't think I was so annoying anymore. And I can't help finding that funny." He shrugs a shoulder. "I still do."

I squeeze his hand, my heart going out to the young boy who felt out of place.

"I work my ass off for this body. No way I could be as good at hockey as I am without being in this kind of shape. But the fact that it makes women think I'm something different, that I'm not that high-energy, chaotic person who exhausts people simply because I look like this? Well, that is still really, really funny to me."

I can picture him, young and mischievous, full of energy. He's still like that, all movement and sharp thought. He's smart, almost lightning quick with his responses, and as much as he might not think so, he's sensitive. He gets people. There's no way that boy, even in the kind of chaotic mess he describes, didn't draw female attention. No way. Declan Mitchell has always stood out in a crowd. I'm sure of it.

"I think you're lying. There's no way you would ever go unnoticed." I place my hands on both sides of his face and look him right in the eyes. "And sure, you're good-looking. Almost ridiculously so. But I think you're the whole package, Declan Mitchell. Smart, funny, and hot."

Something unsteady flashes in his eyes.

To see it there tugs at my heart. "Speaking of packages…" I would have never said something like that to anyone else. I can't even believe I'm saying it here. But it makes him laugh, and that's what I wanted. When I pictured sex, I never expected laughter to have much to do with it. Maybe it doesn't with other guys, but this is Declan.

He cups my face. "We don't have to do anything here, you know. We never have to do anything you don't want to do."

"I want to touch you. Please."

He leans in and kisses me reverently. "I'm all yours."

I shift closer to him on the bed, deepening the kiss. I might be new at this, but I've always been a fast learner. He shudders, and I run my hands across his shoulders. There's strength there, but he watches me like I'm the one with all the power. It emboldens me.

I press against his chest, and he falls back on his elbows. I sweep around to stand between his legs. Dropping my head, I run my tongue over the tattoo that stretches across his chest. He lets his head drop back, and I take that as an invitation to continue in the direction I'm going.

I kiss my way along his muscles, and they flex under my mouth. Splayed out in front of me, he's the sexiest thing I've ever seen. When I take him in my hand, his hips come off the bed.

"Fuck…" He exhales sharply. Then I take him in my mouth, and his eyes flare open.

I drop to kneel in front of him. I have no idea what I'm doing, but I follow his reactions. I'm not completely innocent —I've heard girls talk about this lots of times.

Whatever I'm doing seems to do the trick for him because his fingers fist into the sheets next to him, and his voice takes on a warning timber. "Ivy, sweetheart… you need to stop or… Christ, baby, don't stop. Oh my God, that's…"

My grip tightens on his hips, and that seems to be the end for him. He comes, warm in my mouth, and I swallow him down. As his head falls back and drops to the bed, I feel more powerful than I ever have in my entire life.

He only rests for a moment when he opens and closes his hands a handful of times at me, grabby-hand style. Sweeping forward, he scoops me up and tucks me against him. The feeling of him, curled up behind me, warm and lethargic, is bliss. He tosses the blanket over us and nuzzles his face into the crease of my shoulder.

We doze off, a tangle of limbs.

Ivy

I HEAD BACK TO campus the Wednesday after Declan's game and the night we spent together. I tell myself that it's because Madame Champion asked me to come up with the group dance for the second night of the competition. But Declan's back on campus too. Sure, we need to practice our performances, and I need to work with Madame. After all, the competition is a week and a half away. Still, I won't pretend that's all it is.

I want to see him. It's not complicated.

I have lunch with him before I meet with Madame. The entire time, he pauses to touch my hand or my shoulder, and I swear I lean into him like a cat, looking for pets. I never saw myself as an overtly affectionate kind of person. I'm not standoffish, but the way my body responds to him is a revelation.

I'm almost late for my meeting with Madame. When I get there, I go over my plans for the dance. I give her an overview of the songs and formations I think might work.

"This is impressive, Ivy," she says after I've finished my drafted presentation.

"I'll need to watch everyone after the first competition to make sure I've placed them appropriately, but I think it'll work out well." I try to remain humble, but I'm pretty proud of how it turned out. "I didn't want to devise anything complicated. We don't have a lot of time to learn the routine. I want something fun and entertaining, without a lot of effort on the participants' part." I offer her a sheepish grin. "Besides, some participants are more naturally gifted than others."

"That's very diplomatic." Madame Champion chuckles and places her palms together as she studies me. "I know we have spoken little about your plans after graduation, at least not since you got back. I thought maybe we could do that now, if you have a few moments." She tilts her head. "An opportunity has arisen, and I wanted to discuss it with you."

"Of course." I can't help the flare of excitement that spikes through me. When I spoke with Madame in the fall, I expressed my wish to dance in one of the local troupes. I told her I was open to anything in the Northeast, and even that limitation is only because my parents are both in New York. After the past year, I don't want to stray too far from them.

"I know that in the past, we've discussed your desire to dance with a troupe."

"Yes…" I don't know where this is going.

"But have you ever considered choreography?"

"I'm sorry…" I shake my head. "I'm not sure…" I stop and smile. "What do you mean?"

"Let me start again." She taps on her computer's keyboard before spinning the screen to face me. There's a website open of a beautiful girl with long dark hair. She looks familiar to me, but I can't place her. I cock my head in question to Madame. She continues, "This is Camila Alvarez. She's spent the past semester abroad in Germany. She studied there, but we also approved her to use her acting work on an upcoming major motion film as experiential learning credits."

I'm familiar with experiential learning credits. That's how we have classified some of the dance work I did in New York while I recovered this fall. "A film?"

"Yes. It's an action movie. Something with 'Death' in the title." There's pride in Madame's eyes. "Camila is also a senior. She's on the cusp of stardom, I think."

I'm impressed. A lot of successful students come out of the performing arts department. Declan's friend Hannah Marshall, whom I met on New Year's Eve, will be huge, too. Her debut album is already getting a lot of radio play and is climbing the charts. It speaks to the quality of our professors and staff.

"So Camila is going to be back this last semester?"

"She is." Madame nods. "She mentioned wanting to spend some time in the dance department. I want you to work with her."

"Me?"

"Yes. She has signed on for a leading role in an upcoming musical. Her voice will be fine, but she believes she could use some help with her dance. I would like you to help."

My mouth opens and closes a few times. "Why me?"

"This isn't student work, Ivy," she offers gently, motioning toward my dance plans for the competition. "I've glanced in when you were working with Mr. Mitchell. And I've seen video of some performances you developed in New York. The past six months of your work have been very informed, very mature. Better than anything you've ever exhibited before."

"Thank you, Madame."

"I do not give compliments easily, Miss Deveraux."

I smother a grin. Madame tries to be strict, but she struggles to keep her soft heart concealed. "I am aware, Madame," I say with the straightest face I can manage.

She gives a curt nod. "Please consider what I've suggested. I believe that you and Miss Alvarez would benefit from working together. Your personalities are... in sync, I would say."

I've never met Camila, but I trust Madame's judgment. After all, she had a good feeling about Declan and me. I thank her and request that she email me Camila's information so I can contact her. Madame is more old-fashioned, though. She insists that we all get together in her office after classes begin so that I can meet her.

I agree, and she promises to get in contact with me when Camila gets back from overseas.

As I leave Madame's office, I skip down the hall. I hadn't ever considered that I would be capable of choreography at my age. Usually, dancers need to prove themselves in dance troupes or competition to be taken seriously. But if Madame thinks I'm ready, if she believes I might help this Camila somehow... I'm ready to follow that opportunity.

I twirl, my backpack flapping against my spine, then execute a jump and pirouette, falling into giggles.

Except my head spins, and I lose my balance. I brace myself, palm out, to keep from face-planting into the wall at the top of the stairs. I don't fall, but it's a near miss.

I inhale a few deep breaths, grounding myself. When I'm able, I open my eyes. I haven't had that kind of dizziness in a long time. Since...

Since I got sick.

Heat flashes through me, followed by a cold sweat. That's what terror does—it's chilling and hot at the same time. Even as my body flinches away, I can't pretend. Dizziness. It was one of the first signs.

But normal people get dizzy sometimes. If they don't eat, for example. Or... maybe I haven't been drinking enough water. I've been busy. I traveled to Connecticut, and then I had to hurry and pack to get back on campus for my meeting today. I could be dehydrated.

I rub my eyes and force down my panic, gritting my teeth. When normal people get their dizzy spells, though, they don't immediately assume something is horribly wrong with them. Someday, I hope I can be like them.

Determined to not overreact, I pull my backpack up on my shoulders and hurry down the stairs, heading toward the cafeteria. I promised Declan I'd meet him after practice. Things are going well with him—with everything in my life right now. We're having fun together, we're going to kill this competition, and I could work with Camila by month's end.

Now's the time to just be happy.

Declan

MY PHONE RINGS AS I'm on my way from the rink to meet Ivy for dinner. My agent's name flashes across the screen, and I swipe to answer.

"Howie, how are you?" I haven't heard from him in months, not since we talked over the summer about how I needed to put on a more responsible face with my team. I try not to get excited, but he rarely calls me.

"Declan, I had an interesting call, and I wanted to share it with you."

This sounds more promising than I hoped. "Did you?"

"I just talked to Sidney in Boston. I've been checking in about our buddy Linc, but they asked me about you as well." Howie's Linc's agent too. Linc signed with him after he got drafted out of high school and introduced me to him. Howie and I hoped I'd get picked up in last summer's draft, but after the last game and the negative press... we believe it scared teams off. Hence my leadership role this year.

"Really? And what were they asking about?" I try to keep my words even, but it's hard when I've heard no interest from anyone in a long time.

"Well, they were watching the game on Friday to see how Linc recovered from his groin pull. You guys all played great, but they were impressed with your presence on the ice. They mentioned you look very much in charge of the team right now, more in control, and that the guys seem to look to you as a decision-maker."

I do a silent fist pump, but keep my voice calm. "That's good news."

"It is. This is what we have been hoping for, Declan. Keep it up. I'm going to send some emails and see if I can ratchet up some interest. If Boston noticed you, then other teams will, especially as the season progresses. So keep it up. Maybe we can get you signed as a free agent by year's end. I'll be in touch."

"Thanks. Sounds good."

After we disconnect, I practically skip to the cafeteria, too excited to believe what I just heard. This is everything that I've been hoping for since I started playing ice hockey when I was eight. I haven't ever said out loud that I was worrying that I might not get picked up by an NHL team. I don't believe in putting negative energy into the universe. That doesn't mean that I haven't sometimes, in weak moments, gotten discouraged. Especially last summer, when commentators cast doubts on my ability to benefit a team. I make it a policy to ignore what people say about me. Growing up with my father, people started talking about me—all of my siblings—from a young age. It requires thick skin.

It's hard to ignore talk when actions back it up, though. It wasn't just that commentators were talking about me. The teams agreed with them.

But maybe I've turned a corner. It's not only this call with Howie—it's everything. I haven't been this happy or grounded in a long time.

Ivy's standing outside the cafeteria, huddled in her coat, and her face splits into a wide grin when she sees me. The sight of her hits me in the gut along with the shocking realization that everything—hockey, school, all of it—has been easier and better since her.

That realization unbalances everything inside me, and I misstep, nearly tripping on the stairs on the way up to her. I recover quickly, though. I'm pretty graceful. But I'm still reeling with shock when I get to her side. She looks concerned, glancing at me and the stairs where I almost wiped out. "You okay?"

"Just hurrying to see you." I sweep her up into my arms, twirling her around, allowing her squeals of laughter to soothe me.

"Flirt," she says as I put her back down. But she tilts her head up, and I couldn't keep myself from kissing her if I tried.

"Only with you, Princess," I whisper against her mouth, and as I capture her lips with mine, I realize that's also true. I can't tell if it's our kiss or that truth bomb that makes me lightheaded.

She rolls her eyes at me as we pull away. "You're too much." The way she says it dulls the happiness in my chest.

"I'll show you too much, pretty girl," I whisper in her ear, then nibble at the lobe. She laughs, the sound like bells in my ears, even as she leans into my touch. Right there in front of the cafeteria entrance, in the freezing cold, I know for sure that I am in love with Ivy Deveraux.

It's not only that she's amazingly beautiful, and I can't get enough of her delicious body, though that's part of it. But more than that, it's her laugh and the way she makes me feel inside —calm and happy. Lighter. It's the straightforward way she asks questions and her complete inability to flirt. She laughs at my stupid jokes, and she doesn't take me too seriously. But even in our silent moments, I feel completely at ease in her company. I've never met anyone like this before, and I'm certain I won't again.

I stayed away from her in the beginning because I was afraid I'd hurt her or give her mixed messages. I didn't want her to take this too seriously. Yet here I am, head over heels for her. I'm such an asshole.

I absorb the lines of her face, her cheeks pink from the cold and her gray eyes sparkling with laughter, and I face facts.

Nothing has truly changed. Sure, everything inside me is irrevocably shifted, but our circumstances haven't. I've never done a serious relationship. I'm not even sure I know how. Even if I did, this isn't the right time. Isn't that what the call from Howie just proved? Interest from hockey teams means I'm closer than ever to playing in the NHL. Even if I don't end up in the big leagues, it sounds like I could find a place somewhere.

Who knows where I could end up playing minor-league hockey? I can't make Ivy any promises. I watched my stepmothers and half-siblings deal with my father not being around. Between his extensive travel schedule and the various get-togethers and parties, he's never been reliable. I know how hard that is, and I refuse to do that to someone else. All I can really guarantee is right now.

Except… I'm not the sort of person who treads carefully. If I want something, I dive in, caution be damned. I take chances and accept the risks. Every fiber in my body says that I should do that now—that if I want Ivy, I should just go for it. But if I really love her, I can't be selfish with her.

I inhale and drop another kiss on her lips. She looks confused, but rallies quickly. "Should we go in?"

I nod and follow her. Nothing has changed. She's happy with the current situation, so I should be too.

So why am I already afraid of a future that might not have her in it?

Ivy

I TEACH DECLAN THE Venetian waltz in case we make it to the finals in the competition. If we do, we'll need a third dance number, and I don't want to wait until the last moment to throw something together. Venetian waltzing is a lot faster and more intricate than regular waltzing, but as expected, Declan picks it up with only minor difficulty. I was sure that we could make the dance beautiful, but even I couldn't have guessed how lovely it would feel to have a partner as strong as Declan to handle the sweeps and dips of the dance that I created for us. Again, I stay away from classical songs, instead choosing Ed Sheeran's "Give Me Love." I don't know if I meant to be so obvious with my longing, but as we practice, I realize that's what I did.

I can't help it. We've spent the past week since we arrived back on campus, constantly together. We spend the days when he isn't at practice, either dancing or hanging out. Every night, we end up watching television in his room or talking, and that leads to making out. By the time the first round of the competition arrives, I'm intimately acquainted with every inch of him, but I can't seem to get enough.

I want more. All of him. Sooner than later.

The morning of the competition, I'm confident that we have a good chance of winning this contest. What I'm not as confident about is whatever might be going on in my body. This morning, when I woke up at Declan's place, my clothes were drenched. Maybe I got hot because Declan is such an active sleeper. He sprawls out and rolls around, sometimes even ending up like a starfish in the middle of the bed. Considering that sleeping with him is a contact sport, I wonder if maybe his body heat is why I woke up hot.

But I can't stop the strand of doubt that's creeping into my gut. First, there was the dizziness, and now, a night sweat. I'm trying not to overreact. Normal people don't panic about this stuff. There are a million other possibilities for why I could have been hot last night. It could be... hormones. Who knows?

I push that all aside. It's competition time. I need to focus on our performances, not on doubts and possibilities. Declan has worked hard to make sure that we're successful, and I refuse to let him down by not bringing my A game.

For our first dance, we'll be dancing open-style to the Francis and the Lights' song. After the other partners finish with their first dances, there will be a half hour break in which the audience can text in their votes for their favorite couples. The performing arts department enlisted the help of the computer science department to devise a way to tally the votes accurately. That will allow two different rounds of elimination this evening.

When I leave the girls' dressing room and join Declan in the corridor behind the stage, he looks completely at ease. We avoided bright colors for this dance, but even in his black pants and long-sleeved gray shirt, he's devastatingly handsome.

He leans against the wall, hands in his pockets. I scowl at him. "Don't you suffer from performance anxiety?"

Pushing off, he joins me. "Please. I love to be in front of a crowd."

I shake my head at him, smiling. Of course he does. He leans forward, nuzzling my neck and dropping kisses on the sensitive skin there. I shoo him away. "You're distracting me. I'm trying to get my head in the game here."

He drags me into his arms, cradling me against his body. "You're going to do great. I am completely confident that we are the best couple out there."

I allow my gaze to stray to the other couples milling around. "How do you know that?"

He shrugs. "How could we not be?"

I laugh, but his self-assurance calms my nerves.

The other couples join us, and there's a lot of nervous energy backstage as we wait to go on. The captain of the basketball team is rolling his neck, jumping up and down. I wonder if that's the same process he uses to work out nerves before a big game. The stagehand lines us up, and everyone falls silent, waiting to go on stage for introductions.

Before we got dressed, they explained that, for the beginning, we would all take the stage as a group. Each couple will be called forward for an initial bow. Then we'll wait backstage and be called out separately for our first dance numbers. There are fifteen couples to start, and Declan and I will go fourth. After the first dance, the audience will eliminate five couples. Later tonight, the votes will eliminate five more, leaving five couples for next week's final round.

They wave us all on stage, and Declan and I sweep forward into the bright, hot lights. Declan is a natural in front of an audience. He grins and waves, full of energy. I feed off his charisma, my smile feeling more natural than it ever has in a performance situation. We take our turn around the front of the stage, stopping in the middle to bow. I can't see well in the audience, but I can hear a lot of hooting and hollering. Declan said his entire team plans to come and watch, and judging by the volume, they must be there. I wave in their direction and blow a kiss, which sends up another roar of approval. This is basically a popularity contest. The more crowd support we can drum up, the better.

Backstage again, we wait through the first three dances. The first team, the debate captain and his partner, do a rudimentary cha-cha. When I catch Declan's eye, he raises one shoulder. I'm not impressed either.

The next dance is even more basic, the president of student government and his partner doing a basic waltz. Also, nothing to write home about, and the audience is lukewarm. So far, our chances look good.

But the third dance is the football captain, Roman Ellison. He and Dana manage a foxtrot that even impresses me. When they finish and we're about to take the stage, Roman stops and gives Declan a pat on the shoulder. "Good luck out there. Can't imagine you can do any better than that." As he heads for the dressing room, Declan gives him the finger.

I don't have any time to respond because we're running out onto the stage. The announcer calls our names, and we take our position in the middle of the hardwood. The first strain of our song begins, and after that, same as every time before, I fall under the spell of dancing with Declan.

The audience fades away, and all I see or feel is him. From the very beginning, I've been insanely aware of him. At first, that was unsettling. Now, I lean in, relishing every heady and intoxicating second of being in his arms.

The dance goes off perfectly, and I love every minute of it.

We take our bows and, based on the amount of screaming and noise in front of us, it's clear that we did a pretty good job and the audience enjoyed our performance as much as we did. When things between Declan and me are over, I will always remember this feeling. He reminds me of what it is to be in a moment, to live in my body without overthinking.

We run offstage, and as soon as we're backstage, Declan pulls me into his arms. I laugh as he twirls me around. "We did it." He sounds as triumphant as I feel, and he drops his mouth to mine.

Kissing Declan is like breathing, the most natural movement. As we pull away and I stare into his eyes, I recognize that our time is limited. The competition will be over next Monday, and there's no other reason for things between us to continue. Short term, that's always been the assumption.

If that's the case, if I only have Declan for a short period of time, then tonight I want to make the most of it. I want him. I don't want to pretend any longer that I don't, and I don't want to deny it. I don't want to always wonder what would have happened, what the experience would be like with him.

I pull his face back to mine, and he doesn't need much coaxing to kiss me again.

Declan

AS EXPECTED, IVY AND I move on to the second round. Of course, Roman Ellison isn't eliminated either. Dickhead.

I watched all the first dances, though, and I still feel good about our chances at winning this entire thing. As Ivy and I wait for the second dance of the night, she doesn't say much. She's been quiet since our first dance. I'm trying to give her some space. I don't have performance anxiety, but maybe she does more than she was letting on.

We do our salsa to Michael Franti and Spearhead's "Say Hey (I Love You)." As we make our way through the dance, I can hear people clapping along to the music and singing it back to us. I feed off that shit. Ivy's as sparkling as ever, and we nail our routine. When the music stops, the cheers could bring down the house. We smile and bow, waving as we run off the stage.

We were the last to perform, but I'm amped up afterward. We won't know until sometime later tonight or tomorrow morning if we'll make it into the final round. The adrenaline rush is like playing a big hockey game, though, and I work it off the same as I do in those cases—I talk out all the details, go over all the highlights.

"That dip that we added into the salsa,"—I give a chef's kiss —"I have no idea how you can see the ways the different parts of a routine come together like you do, but you're phenomenal."

She smiles, but it's shy. We're in my car, driving to her door. Now that she's back on campus as a full-time student, she's been given full residence at the Covenant Apartments, lovingly referred to as the "Convent" because it's a girls' only dorm.

The rooms there are nice, have kitchenettes, and are close to the main buildings, so it's a good living situation. When I pull up out front, she doesn't immediately get out. In the passenger seat, she wrings her hands and bites her bottom lip between her teeth.

She's upset about something. Whatever it is, it's unacceptable. "What's up, Princess?"

"Would you be able to stay the night?"

"Are you asking me for a booty call?" I tease her, but I'm already looking around on the street for parking. I find a space and quickly parallel park. If my girl wants quality time, that's what she'll have.

"Yes." She glances up at me. There's a streetlight nearby, so I can see her gray eyes clearly. There's a decided glint there. "A real one."

"What are we talking about?" I'm afraid that I'm reading this differently than she intends, or maybe I'm trying too hard not to hope. I need clarification. I leave the car running, but I've gone completely still behind the wheel. "A real what?"

"I want you. Tonight. All of you." She swallows, and I watch her delicate neck work. "I want to sleep with you."

"Sleep? Or have sex with me?"

Even in the near dark of the car, I can see her blush. "The second part. The sex."

"I…" I'm not sure where I'm going with that. Everything inside of me is screaming for her. I've never wanted anyone as much as I want Ivy, never felt as strong about someone as I feel about her.

Since we've returned to campus, we've spent a lot of time together. At first, it was under the guise of practicing for the competition. Those sessions ended with us making out. After we had mastered our dances, we couldn't use that as an excuse any longer. Turned out that we didn't need an excuse. We both wanted to hang out, so we did. A lot of times, we made out, too, but it's more than that. I enjoy Ivy's company. I enjoy hearing all her thoughts and getting her opinions on things.

When classes started, we met at the library to work together. She started sitting at the table with the hockey team at lunch. My New York Rangers were on a winning streak, and we watched some of their games together, curled up on the couch in her apartment, our arms and legs twisted together. I've always been a physical guy, but I can't seem to get enough of touching her skin.

Over the past two weeks, I've learned so much about her body, the touches she likes, the things she doesn't. It's not enough, though. No matter how much it is, it's never enough.

We haven't had sex. It's not that I haven't wanted to because that's not it. Every instinct in me has cried out for her, but it's remained an unspoken line in the sand that we haven't crossed yet.

I admit—I'm scared. The stronger my feelings have become for her, the more afraid I am. It's supposed to hurt the first time, and I can't bear the thought of causing Ivy pain in that way. Not only that, but what if she regrets it afterward and decides that I was a mistake? In the past, all I've cared about is what happened at the moment. If my bedmate was having fun in the sheets, I didn't care what happened later. I was up-front with my intentions, so any emotional fallout was never my responsibility.

Now, how I feel for Ivy stretches out in front of me—how sex might change our relationship, how it might change how she sees me. And I'm terrified at how much deeper it will make me fall for her.

I attempt to work up a response, but the pressure in my chest is too heavy, and no words squeeze out.

She interrupts whatever nonsense I might have said, though, holding her hand up. "Before you say anything, yes... I am completely aware of how this will go. You're casual, short term, and I'm okay with that. I'm not looking for any commitment from you. I know who you are, and I recognize that we're about to graduate in a couple of months and our futures are completely different. But I know what I want, and I've never wanted anything as much as I want to be with you that way tonight."

I stare out the windshield, gripping the steering wheel so tightly that I'm afraid I'll rip it off the dash. Everything she said is so off base, so opposite of everything that I feel right now, that it's almost painful to not correct her.

Except what can I say? I don't know how to be anyone's forever, and we both know it. But I can't stay away from her either. I don't want to. I fucking love this girl. There's no way I can say no to her. If she wants this from me, then I'll give her all that I have.

Besides, no one will take as much care of her through this as I will. I'm certain, and that soothes some of my fears.

When I face her, I hate the uncertainty in her expression. It's like a punch in the gut. I reach out, running my thumb along her lower lip. Her eyes flutter closed, and I want to drink in the shaky sigh that escapes her mouth.

"Pretty girl, I'm all yours," I say. "Whatever you want from me, you can have." Though there are a million more things that are on the tip of my tongue—feelings, emotions—I swallow them down.

I shouldn't make promises I don't know if I can keep.

Ivy

MY HAND SHAKES AS I slip the key into the lock on my room. Inside, I take in my studio. It's not as neat as I'd prefer. I was running around before our performance, grabbing last-minute things, so the room has a lived-in feel about it. I sweep in and start tidying, tossing discarded clothes into a pile.

"Ivy." Declan's voice stops me. I face him, my arms full of laundry. "Are you going to clean?" There's teasing in his expression but also tenderness. He opens his arms. "Come here."

I drop my armload and step into his embrace. He folds himself around me, and his warmth seeps through me. I relax, and I hadn't even realized how tense I was. I curve my arms around him.

We stand in the middle of my room, for a long time, holding each other. I hadn't realized how nervous I was, but apparently, he did. But the longer we stand there, pressed together, the more aware I am of how much I need more than this. I want to touch him. I want to be close to him, closer than I've been to anyone.

I lean back to meet his eyes. "Declan?"

"Yeah?"

I give him a teasing side-eye. "I swear, if we are just going to cuddle…"

He chuckles and squeezes me in his arms. "I have never met anyone so hateful to cuddling." I giggle, and he sweeps me into his arms. The movement happens so quickly that it steals my breath and my ability to relax. Now, everything in me vibrates, and I'm trapped in the intensity of his eyes.

Declan's dipped me, tossed me, and twirled me in dance after dance, but this is so much different from that. Here, he's not only holding me, but he's also pressing me against him.

It's only a handful of steps to get to my bed, and he deposits me in the center of it slowly. I glance down. Nothing about my outfit is sexy. After a quick post-competition shower, I threw on the sweatpants and oversized sweatshirt I wore to the theater earlier. My hair probably looks the same as always. One positive of having short hair is that it dries quickly. I worry my lip with my teeth. Maybe I should have planned this differently. Tomorrow, we could have gone out for dinner. I could have worn nicer underwear than the sports bra and cotton panties I'm currently sporting.

"I have no idea what's going on inside your head." Declan interrupts my internal wardrobe criticism, and I meet his gaze. "Whatever it is, I need to help you stop it."

I pull at my sweatshirt, spreading it out so that he can see the faded Chesterboro logo on the front. "This is not seductive attire."

He allows his gaze to sweep over me. There's heat in his heavy-lidded appraisal, and I force myself not to squirm. When his eyes return to mine, anything lighthearted has faded. "Ivy, you could wear anything, and I'd still find you the most beautiful, the sexiest, and the most perfect woman I've ever seen."

His words warm me. Not because I'm embarrassed or shy, but because I feel them, deep in my chest. Any self-consciousness fades, and I narrow my eyes at him. "A clown costume?"

He grins and winks at me. "I think you'd make a sexy clown."

I burst out laughing, and he lowers beside me, gathering me close, and places his lips on mine. What starts as a teasing kiss becomes hot almost immediately, though. I lace my fingers in his hair, tugging him closer and arching into his body.

I can barely remember a time when I haven't wanted Declan Mitchell. He discarded his hoodie when he got here, so now I've only got the T-shirt he wore under it standing between me and his warm skin. I tug at the hem, and he shifts, pulling at the neck, dragging it over his head.

My fingers play along his chest, tracing the lines of his tattoos. I'm intimately acquainted with all of them. I've put my mouth on them and allowed my fingers to trace them. I doubt I'll ever get enough of his skin—its taste, its warmth, the intoxicating smell of him. But most of all, it's the way he moves with me, the way he curls his body into my touch. I might be hyper-aware of him, but I am certain he is hyper-aware of me too. The chemistry between us has always been electric.

"Ivy…" He reaches for my shirt. What follows is the kind of quick disrobing that I imagine Superman might employ. We're out of our clothes in record time. When we come back together, skin to skin, I gasp, and he lets out a groan. "Fuck… you feel so good. All the time. Every time. I…" He swallows, meeting my gaze. "I can't..." He shakes his head, running a finger along my cheek, down my collarbone, and to my right breast. My breathing hitches. "I can't... won't ever get enough of you."

His words sing through me, but I'm sure he doesn't mean them the way I wish he did. My heart would love to hear anything that hints at forever. But that's not what we're dealing with here. We're a snapshot in time, perfect right now. I refuse to allow myself to breathe more meaning into it than that, because if I do, I'm sure that will only lead to pain later.

I can't think of that. We're here, and it feels right. That's all I plan to focus on.

I reach for him, pulling his face to mine, and he takes my mouth in a hungry kiss. From there, it's like he can't get enough of me. I swear, he kisses every inch of my body, allows his fingers to find all the sensitive spots. He leaves the center of me for last, though, and by the time his mouth finds me there, I am desperate and panting, arching into him.

I'm so turned on that only a few kisses there have me tumbling over the edge and into a sparkling orgasm. When I'm coming down, I open my eyes to find Declan poised between my legs, his gaze hot. I reach up to cup his cheek, and he closes his eyes, pressing his face into my hand.

"Ivy, if you have any doubts about this, I need you to say so." He shifts, dropping two quick kisses on my palm. When his gaze meets mine again, it's pleading. "It might hurt. I don't know how much. I'm not a small guy, and I don't know how this is going to feel for you. So, if there's any reason that you aren't sure you want to go forward, please... tell me now."

I cup his face, dragging his mouth back down to mine. He growls against my lips, and I feel the sound deep in my stomach. I would have thought that after one orgasm, my body would be tired. But I feel the pressure rising in me again. My senses are overwhelmed by him, but I've never felt more certain about anything in my life. "I want to do this with you, Declan. Please."

He nods, then he shifts, leaning over the side of the bed. Plastic crinkles. Right, a condom. That's necessary. He's back in a split second, though, poised between my open thighs. His hot gaze follows the lines of me, and my desire amps up further. He grips my hips in his hands, and I can feel him trembling. His brow is low, and he's laser-focused on my body. I pant, my heart thundering as I wait for whatever is going to happen next. But he's slow and deliberate.

"God, Ivy... I don't know what I'm doing..."

I press a finger to his lips, and his eyes meet mine again. His face is open, completely vulnerable, and it steals what's left of my ability to breathe. Any nervousness I might have been feeling leaves me. This man... I've chosen the right man to share this with.

"It's okay," I whisper. "Be here with me."

He holds my gaze, and some of the turmoil in his eyes fades. He shifts forward, and I jump a bit when I feel him pressed against the opening of me. Then I'm shaking, waiting, as he runs the head of himself against me a few times. Slowly, he pushes forward the slightest bit, sliding inside me.

He pauses, panting, and when I run my fingers along his shoulders, there's sweat and tension there. "More, Declan," I gasp out. "Please."

"I need to go slow," he grits out. "I need..."

Impatiently, I shift my hips. Not much, but an inch or so, and he slides farther inside me. A moan escapes me and he growls, his eyes squeezing closed. "Please, sweet girl, please. Just… give me a second."

I get the impression that he's struggling to hold on to his control, but everything feels frantic inside my body, and I don't want to hold still any longer. I want to move and I want to feel. I want whatever is hovering in front of me, waiting. "Declan," I rasp, "I need you. Just please. Come inside me."

His jaw firms, and his body is shaking with barely contained tension. He opens his eyes, and I see a determined glint there. "Ivy, I'm so sorry if this hurts you."

"I don't care. Please. Move."

He pushes forward, holding my hips. He's not rough, only insistent. He holds my eyes the entire time, and I refuse to flinch, to make him second-guess any of this, even when the discomfort makes me shift my weight.

There's no sharp flash of pain like some girls describe, but Declan's large. He stretches me farther than I ever imagined, and the tightness and sting of it are foreign. He continues, pushing inside me for long moments until he presses the last fraction forward with a jerk that makes me whimper, despite my determination to remain quiet for him.

But the pressure is so much, and I squirm, attempting to adjust to it.

"Ivy, please don't move. God, baby, you're so tight, and I'm dying here…" He's begging, his entire body rigid above me. I breathe through the discomfort, but even as I brace myself for it, it's fading, leaving only the feel of him inside me, where there had only ever been emptiness without him.

I roll my hips forward the slightest fraction, expecting pain, but there's only pleasure now, and that exotic too-full feeling.

The movement sets off friction that sends a heady buzz of bliss through my lower stomach. I sigh. "Declan, can you…"

He runs his finger along my hairline. "What?"

"I think it will feel good if you move now?"

He leans forward to kiss me softly, and that movement alone makes me whimper again, but this time with need, not with unease. He pulls out of me a bit, and I miss him, but then he pushes forward, and I cry out.

He stops. "Are you okay?"

"I'm perfect. Do that again."

He chuckles and does as I ask. He sets up a steady rhythm and I'm lost. I would have never imagined that this could feel this good. But Declan's presence in my body feels like I've found a missing piece that has returned home. Every movement sends me higher, spiraling up and up toward some emotion that I crave, but I can't name. He increases his tempo, like he knows exactly where we're going, and I trust him to get us there.

When my orgasm poises over me, he reaches between us and rubs my clit with soft and sure fingers, and I explode, crying out his name. My body grips at him, and the feeling deep inside me only intensifies the waves of euphoria washing over me. He increases his pace again, and it makes me cry out once more. This time, though, he stiffens and calls out my name. I watch him, overcome by his own emotions, and I realize that what I feel for him is more than something short term.

There won't ever be someone else like Declan. Not for me. Never.

When he calms, he gently retreats from inside me, and I immediately miss him. But he pulls my sweaty body against him, and we doze off like that, in perfect sync.

Declan

THERE ARE TWO WEEKS between the dance competitions. The Friday after the first one, our game is back at home. Ivy sits in my seat in the players' section again, but this time, she's wearing my away jersey. It's always been a thing among the team and the puck bunnies who hang out with us. When a guy is in a relationship with a girl, he will give her his jersey to wear to home games. I've always thought it was cheesy. But I can't deny how much I enjoy seeing her slight form swallowed up in my clothes, my number on her back as she watches me.

Not as much as I like seeing her in my bed without clothes, though.

This week has been a revelation. Sex with Ivy is like nothing I've ever felt before. I've told her that too. No matter how many ways I try to say it, though, I get the impression that she thinks I'm only flattering her.

I'm not. I've never felt so close and connected with anyone before. It's exhilarating and terrifying.

Tonight, as always, her presence settles me. I don't have the same desire to go off the playbook, and I hold it together. I don't know if working with her has taught me truly how to be part of a team, but whatever the reason, my game has never been as solid.

The rest of the guys follow suit. We focus on the basics, and it's an easy win. We're in the lead in our division. The locker room is jubilant, the guys patting each other on the back and taking credit for their work out on the ice. I joke around with them, but I don't linger after my shower. I want to see Ivy, and I know she's outside, waiting for me.

What I don't expect when I get out into the hall is to find my father surrounded by a small group of people. He sees me, though, and cuts through the crowd to pull me into a hug. "Hey, buddy. You played really great out there." He pats me on the back and smiles. Like always, my father's a huge personality, taking up a lot of space in the crowded corridor. But I can't help but look over his shoulder, keeping my eye out for Ivy.

I don't see her as I shake my father's hand. "I didn't know you were coming to the game." My father isn't at a lot of my games, but he tries to show up for a couple every year. Usually, he would have given me some warning. I wonder what explains his unannounced appearance.

"I didn't have any hard plans this weekend, and it's been a while since I've been out to Chesterboro. I thought today was a nice day for a drive. And I'm glad I did. What a game. You played great." He looks me over, and I can't help but grin at the pride on his face. My father's not a bad guy. In fact, he has always financially supported my half-siblings and me. He's affectionate when he's around, he doesn't yell, and he isn't a harsh disciplinarian. He's just not around much, and he doesn't follow through all the time.

"It's good to see you," I say, and I mean it. "I just didn't expect to see you so soon. You were here right before Thanksgiving."

He shrugs, glancing around at the crowd and the stadium. "This is your last year. I want to make sure I get here a few different times before this is all over for you. I mean, after this, who knows where I'll be traveling to see you play? That agent of yours—Howie, right?"

I nod.

"Who knows where Howie's going to get you settled? You told him to keep it close, right? Along the east coast would be great for your mom and me." He winks at me. Sometimes, it's uncanny how much we look alike.

I roll my eyes. "As if I control that, Dad. You know how this works."

He gives me a side hug. "I can hope, can't I?" When he drops his arm, I notice a woman standing nearby. She steps closer, and I realize that she's there with my father.

My smile fades as I take her in. She's not what I expect. She's young, even for him, and she's flashy. Her hair is harshly dyed, and she's wearing a lot of makeup. Mostly, she looks starstruck by him. He motions to her, and she curls into his side.

"Declan, this is Sherry. She was nice enough to come along with me for the drive today."

"Nice to meet you, Sherry," I say, folding the hand she proffers in my own. I'm not about to be rude to her. But she's the one that surprises me—her eyes run up and down my body in one of the most thorough and audacious physical inspections I've ever received.

I pull my hand back, my smile fading and my good mood souring.

"What are you up to tonight?" He asks as he gives Sherry a side squeeze. "I thought maybe I could take you out for a drink or a bite to eat."

I glare at him. "May I speak with you for a moment?" I ask, motioning out of Sherry's hearing distance. "Just over there." I nod to her, my expression mild. "Excuse us for just a minute. I'll have him right back with you." I clutch my father's elbow and we step aside.

I keep my voice low to avoid anyone overhearing us. "Dad, what the hell? Who is this girl? She doesn't look like she's that much older than I am." I glance back to where Sherry's openly checking out some of my teammates. "Your divorce with Pam isn't even final yet. Maybe let the ink dry on the document before you drive new women around and introduce them to your kids."

He has the decency to look sheepish. "I wouldn't introduce her to the younger ones." He waves off his discomfort, giving me another smile. "It's not like that, anyway. She's nothing serious. But I mentioned I was going to see you, and she offered to keep me company."

"I bet she did."

His brows drop. "Be kind, Declan. I'm not getting any younger."

"That doesn't mean that you should run right out and find a girlfriend before you're even properly divorced." I shake my head. "You know what? I have plans this evening." Over his shoulder, I catch sight of Ivy waiting a safe distance away, trying not to intrude on my conversation. "Why don't you and

Sherry go ahead out for dinner on your own. I have somewhere I have to be."

My father follows my gaze and takes Ivy in. "Your plans have anything to do with that girl?"

"That has nothing to do with you." I don't want to talk about Ivy with him. She's different, special. Better than both of us. Introducing her to my father feels wrong, and I don't need to change my plans to suit him. I certainly don't have to share the girl who's made me happier than I've ever been before with him.

He pauses. My father has always been good at reading a situation. He obviously doesn't want to pick a fight with me because he nods. "I'll be staying in town tonight. Why don't we get together in the morning for breakfast?"

I quash my irritation. It's not his fault that he's like this. Or rather, he's been like this my entire life. He probably doesn't even realize that he's doing anything inappropriate. "That sounds fine. Text me and we'll meet up."

"Good. I'll see you in the morning." He slaps me on the shoulder. When my father says "morning," he really means lunchtime.

He and Sherry wander away, and Ivy joins me. I fold her into my arms, allowing her presence to soothe me.

She shifts back to look at me. "Was that your father?"

It's only then that I realize my misstep. "It was. I'm sorry, I should have introduced you." Why didn't I think about how she would feel if I didn't?

There's a brief flash of hurt in her eyes before she smiles too brightly. "No, it's not a big deal at all. He obviously had company." She offers an offhand wave, but she's not meeting my eyes. "I'm sure it must annoy you, having everyone want to meet him all the time."

"No, Ivy…" I take her hands, gripping her icy fingers in mine. "That's not it. He's just… difficult, and I didn't want…"

"You seriously don't need to explain anything to me, Declan." She squeezes back. "I get it. I'm sure you don't want to keep introducing him to the girls you're sleeping with."

The words are a kick in my stomach. That's not how this is. I mean, she's not wrong. I wouldn't introduce him to just any girl. But she isn't just a girl… she's more important to me than that.

I sift through my mind, trying to figure out how to explain the dynamic with my father. To me, my father is a cautionary tale. He's famous and wealthy, but he's all flash and no substance. I don't want to be him, and I certainly don't want her to meet him and start noting all the similarities between us. I want her to see me as better than that.

"That's not it. Ivy, you're not like any of…" I begin, searching for how to make this right when Griff and Ash step out of the locker room.

"Mitch, you coming?" Griff calls.

She tugs my hand, pulling me toward the exit. "Come on. Let's get going. Everyone else is already headed to Shepherd." She hurries me along as if the conversation is forgotten. At least, she seems to forget it.

As I follow her out of the building, I'm left thinking it's ironic that the first time I want something more with someone, she seems completely content with the status quo.

Ivy

CAMILA IS NOT WHAT I expect. She's so down to earth, I wouldn't have guessed she's an up-and-coming movie star. If anything, she's almost overly friendly. We get together in one of the studios the Wednesday before the final dance competition, and I ask her how she's adjusting to being back.

Her smile is full of sunshine. "Totally different from being on a set and shooting." She laughs. "But it's nice to have all my stuff in one spot. Oh, and to not have to sleep in a cold trailer." She wrinkles her nose and shakes her head.

I never considered what it must be like to live like that for any length of time. Movie-making sounds so glamorous. What she describes, not so much.

I change the subject. "I'm really excited to work with you this semester. Madame Champion said that you were going to be doing an independent study, improving your dancing for a part, and you wanted me to choreograph with you."

"My manager recommended some choreographers. They would create the routines, and I would learn them, expand my skills. But I would like to have more input on the overall aesthetics, to really deep-dive into the mechanics. I want to learn about it. That means working more closely with and choosing my own choreographers." She exhales a frustrated sigh then waves and smiles. "Anyway, Madame said you're extremely talented, and she forwarded me some of your performance videos. I really think that it'll be a lot of fun to work with you."

"I agree." We share a grin, and I decide that we're going to get along well. "I'm just back on campus after a year away, so if you want to go out, call me. That way, we can get to know each other better. Right now, I'm spending a lot of time with the hockey team." I shrug. "I'm kind of, sort of dating the captain, Declan." I'm not sure if that's the right way to explain what's happening between us, but "friends with benefits," or "systematic booty calling," feel awkward and wordy.

"Declan Mitchell?" Her eyes widen. "I'm not sure I've ever heard of him dating anyone."

I'm immediately uncomfortable. After all, I don't know if he would ever call it dating. We're hanging out, we're friends, and we've slept together. In fact, we've slept together more than a few times now. Remembering those times, my face heats, and I'm sure I'm blushing.

I assumed that sex with Declan was going to be amazing, but I never expected just how life-changing it would be for me. In his arms, I feel safe, beautiful, and cherished. Not to mention the pleasure. He knows exactly how to drag out every emotion. It's heavenly. He left this morning to go to Philadelphia for a meeting with the Tyrants' general manager. Tomorrow, he'll be in Boston to meet with the Gladiators.

I hate how much I'm going to miss him, even though it's only a couple of days. That isn't the stuff of casual relationships. I need to get a grip. After all, at his game this weekend, he didn't want to introduce me to his father. If anything was going to remind me we're not serious, that was it.

"Oh, it's nothing serious," I finally say, even though the words sting somewhere soft inside me. I shift in my seat and glance around, trying to keep it light. "We're just having some fun." As the words escape, I force myself to bury just how much I wish it was more than that.

"I can understand that." Her eyes get faraway, almost wistful. "My old boyfriend played hockey. Still does, just not here."

"The hockey guys that I've met all seem really nice. I can introduce you, if you like. Linc Reynolds is dating a friend of mine, but Declan's other roommates are both single, as far as I know. Ash Draper and Griffin Parker."

If it's possible for a person's face to drain of color, then that's what I watch happen to Camilla. "I'm sorry. What did you say their names were?"

I'm not sure what I said that upset her, but I repeat myself. "Ash Draper and Griffin Parker?"

"Ash Draper isn't here." She shakes her head, closing her eyes. "He's in Florida."

"Do you know Ash?" I ask gently because it's obvious that something is very wrong between her and Ash.

"Ash is my old boyfriend. We dated in high school, but he's a year behind me in school. We grew up about forty-five minutes from here. I applied to Chesterboro so I could stay close to him. We planned he would join me here and play for the Bulldogs hockey team." She drops her gaze, wringing her hands in her lap. "But when it came time for him to graduate, he didn't follow. He went to play juniors in Canada for a year, and then he played for a college team in Florida. What is he doing here?"

I don't know the answers to those questions. All my experiences with Ash led me to believe that he was a decent guy. My new friend looks distraught, though, so I lean over and give her a hug. Being around Declan so much has turned me into a real hugger. "I guess you might not want me to introduce you to Declan's roommate, then."

"Hell no." She snorts. "Ash and I said what we needed to say a couple of years ago. If Ash is here to play hockey, that's wonderful for him. I wish him the best. But that has nothing to do with me. He made his priorities clear back then. Nothing has changed." The finality in her voice makes me almost feel bad for Ash. As far as I can tell, he seems like a nice enough guy, but I don't know what happened between the two of them. It's not my place to say.

"Well, the offer still stands. If you want to go out for a drink sometime, just drop me a text. We can avoid the hockey boys."

She laughs, and any shadow from our talk about Ash fades from her face. "That sounds like fun, but I don't really go out much. I'm more of a stay-at-home, bake cookies, and watch a movie kind of friend."

I smile. "That sounds like heaven to me."

"Then you have a date," she says, grinning back.

I shift from where I'm sitting on the ground so that I can get up. A wave of dizziness washes over me, making me freeze to where I'm kneeling on hands and knees in the middle of the studio. I close my eyes against a wave of nausea. "Whoa."

"Are you okay?" Camilla asks. I close my eyes and shake my head, doing my best to orient myself. I force myself to laugh and play it off, even though this isn't at all amusing. "It's nothing. I probably just got up too fast." Slowly, I shift to stand, careful to make sure I have my balance. I change the subject to deflect from my dizzy spell. "How about we plan to get together at the beginning of next week? By then, I should have some thoughts on the music samples you sent me. We'll be able to talk more about what you're looking to do and how I can help."

"That sounds great. I'll see you then. And I'll drop you a text this weekend, if you're going to be around."

"I will. I've got practice for the final dance competition on Monday." Not only have Declan and I planned to get together to fine-tune our final number, but we also have a couple of practices with all the participants. I organized a meeting a few days ago to go over the details of the full cast number I wrote, but we still need a bit more practice.

"The Dance Across the Campus competition?"

I laugh. "Yeah, that's the one. Declan and I are partners, and we made it to the final round with four other pairs. I think we have a good chance of winning the whole thing."

"It's on Monday night? I will definitely have to come and watch you guys win." She squeezes my arm, and I pat her hand.

"That sounds great." We say our goodbyes, and I head to the restroom before leaving the building.

In front of the mirror, I stare at my reflection before splashing some cold water on my face. That's my second bout of dizziness. Add that to the night sweats I've had on a couple of occasions, and it's time for me to get serious. As much as I don't want to admit it, it might be time for me to get some blood work.

I fish my phone out of my purse as I push out of the bathroom and into the hallway. I sit on one of the plush chairs in the vestibule and call my oncologist. When the nurse picks up, I say, "Good afternoon. Could you please patch me through to the referral line? I would like to have some bloodwork done. And I'd like to set up an appointment to go over the results with Dr. Proctor on Friday."

I just told Camila that I'd be around this weekend, but apparently, my body has decided I need to make other plans.

Declan

I DRIVE TO PHILADELPHIA on the Wednesday before our last competition to meet with the Tyrants. Howie flies in from New York for the day, and then we fly together to Boston that afternoon.

Wednesday night, I send Ivy a text to see how her meeting with Camila went. This morning, she was really excited about it all, going on about how it could be a really great experience and a strong addition to her portfolio.

But the responses she sends back are short. Then she tells me she'll be going home tomorrow night, that something came up with her parents or something, and she needs to skip classes on Friday. She doesn't give many details, and I'm not sure how to ask without sounding like I'm overreacting. I wish her a good night, and we sign off.

My Thursday morning meeting with the Gladiators in Boston goes well—at least Howie seems to think so, based on his enthusiasm when we sit down for lunch before we both catch separate flights home.

"I'm really excited about both opportunities for you. I think that the team in Boston might offer you a better contract, but you might have more playing time in Philadelphia. We'll have to see what they come back with." Howie is two drinks in and has gotten chatty.

I try to match his enthusiasm. "That sounds really great. How long do you think it will be before we know?" It's the right question to ask. I'm supposed to care about all the details of my contracts, but I can't help worrying about Ivy. She hasn't texted me all day. I hope everything is okay with her and her parents. A million different scenarios cross my mind. Did someone get hurt? If so, she would have told me, wouldn't she? Maybe she's out of cell range. She didn't give too many details about what her plans were for the day.

"Who knows?" Howie shrugs. "We could hear something next week, or they could wait through the playoffs. Some of it's going to depend on where their standings are this year and if they go into the post-season or not. But I still think that this is encouraging." He calls the server over. "Are you sure you don't want a drink?"

I shake my head. In an hour or so, I'll be flying back to Philadelphia, and then I'll need to drive the two and a half hours back to Chesterboro. Besides, I'm not really in the mood to celebrate.

We chat through another drink for Howie, then head to the airport. After we check in, then separate after security, I'm left with about half an hour before boarding with nothing to do.

I read through my text thread with Ivy. She's been quiet all week. Is she second-guessing taking our physical relationship a step further? Even the possibility fills me with dread because sex with Ivy was better than anything I've ever experienced before.

Even as I worry, that doesn't make sense. She was fine after that. We had sex again on Tuesday night. Twice. All of it has been amazing, mind-blowing.

No, something must have happened yesterday.

Concern mixes with frustration. If something happened, why didn't she tell me? Even as I consider the question, I know the answer. We're supposed to be all fun and hookups. If she thinks that's all I want, she might not think that I want to know about important things going on with her.

I bite the inside of my lip. That's my fault. I've let this go on too long. I should have told her how I really felt about her days ago, as soon as I knew. I've never been cautious or hesitant about anything, but with Ivy, I'm terrified. I can't leave things like this. Pretending to see her casually... it's opened a pit in my chest. I don't pretend well. I dive in and take risks. But if I move forward and try to make a genuine commitment to her, I'm almost positive I'm going to fuck it all up.

I guess I believed she would understand. I've spent nearly every spare moment with her. She's the person I want to talk to first thing in the morning and the last one I want to see at night. There's nothing casual about any of that.

Everything has become so confusing. Two months ago, if anyone had told me I would be stressing about whether a girl was texting me back, I would have laughed. But here I am, overthinking everything as I stare at my phone.

I'm just going to call her. I open her contact and dial. After a series of rings, I drop into her voicemail.

I try to keep my concern out of my voice, but I'm pretty sure that's a failure. "Hey, sweet girl. Haven't heard much from you and just wanted to make sure everything's okay. I just finished with my meetings in Boston. Both days' trips seem to have been successful. At least that's what Howie says, and he would know better than I would." I pause, collecting my thoughts.

"Do me a favor and call me back when you have a few minutes. I miss your voice."

It's not "I love you," but it's as close as I can get on a voicemail. I disconnect, then pocket my phone. But she doesn't return my call by the time I board. When I land in Philadelphia, I have no voicemails or texts.

In fact, I don't hear from her for the rest of the night.

Ivy

I HEAR MY PHONE vibrate in my purse. Absently, I snag it out and see Declan's name on the screen. I stare at it but don't answer.

In front of me, my oncologist, Dr. Proctor, is explaining the results of my blood work. "Some of your levels are up. That leads us to believe that you have some inflammation or infection of some sort." She keeps her voice professional and matter-of-fact, but I can see the sympathy in her eyes.

I hate it.

"I've already put it into our scheduler. She's set you all up. We'll send you over to the imaging center next. They'll run some more tests and get a better look at what's going on."

My mother leans forward. There's fear and panic in her expression, but I can tell she's doing her best to keep her voice calm. "When you say, 'inflammation or infection,' that could just be a regular cold or something, correct?" She glances at me for confirmation, but my throat is tight, and I can't answer her. "There are a lot of other reasons for unusual blood count levels."

"Absolutely." The doctor says, but it sounds placating.

"This doesn't mean that she's having a recurrence." Mom sits back and wraps her arms around herself. Her foot taps a manic beat against the floor.

"It does not," my doctor allows, "but we can't rule that out without additional testing.

My mother opens her mouth as if she's going to argue. I hold up my hand to stop her. She's an attorney, so in her professional life, whoever makes the more valid point wins. But this is science and medicine. No matter what she says, it will not change the facts.

There's a significant chance that my cancer is back. No amount of arguing is going to change that.

"I understand completely, Dr. Proctor. You're saying that there's a chance it could be something else, but these numbers aren't encouraging." I restate the current conclusions to make sure that Dr. Proctor knows I get it. Saying the words out loud makes it feel more tangible, though, and I need to take a deep breath to calm my racing heart.

Dr. Reynolds closes her eyes and shakes her head. "I'm not ready to say anything. These tests are inconclusive, and when we have imaging and some more extensive tests, we should know more." The finality in her voice says that's all she's willing to give right now, and I nod.

We gather our paperwork and belongings before we head for the door. Dr. Proctor promises to be in touch as soon as she gets the results from the testing I'm heading off to do. She suggests that she might have news for us as early as Monday. My mother and I thank her for her time, then leave.

I listen to my mom talk the entire way down the elevator and out onto the street. She considers that the blood work numbers are wrong. She supposes that I have the flu or something. I don't tell her I'm not really congested, no more than with allergies, and I don't have any other flu-like symptoms. She doesn't want to hear anything like that right now. She's not really talking to me, after all. She's trying to convince herself that there's nothing to panic about.

But I'm way past that already. I've been panicking for a week. I don't tell her that, though.

As I lay awake last night, I couldn't help but take stock of every detail of my health these past couple of weeks. Besides the two bouts of dizziness and the night sweat, I've been tired. I attributed it to spending too many late nights in Declan's bed. Now, I can't help but wonder if that's linked to this.

I was exhausted before my original diagnosis as well.

Dr. Proctor's office is on a side street in Manhattan. Here, on the sidewalk, I pause to look around. There are people heading out to lunch. They're walking quickly—most New Yorkers do, I think—talking on their phones or listening to music.

They're all living their lives. I'm sure they've got trials, though, things they're struggling with. Maybe they're even worse than what I'm going through.

"Ivy, are you even listening to me right now?"

I sigh and attempt to smile at my mother. "Yes. You are considering all the ways this might not be a big deal."

She blinks at me. "Well, yes."

"I know." My grin feels sad. "We need to be at the imaging place in an hour. Did you want to grab something to eat before that?"

We're in the middle of the sidewalk. Pedestrians need to shuffle around us, but both of us ignore their pointed glances. My mother opens her arms, and I step into them. We stand there, hugging each other, for longer than what's polite on a public street in downtown New York.

"Come on," my mom says, pulling away. "Let's grab a bite."

My phone vibrates in my pocket again, this time with a text. Declan. There's a text and a voicemail he left earlier. I step out of sidewalk traffic to listen.

His voice calms me, but I close my eyes, bracing myself against that. I'm barely holding myself together. My throat thickens as I finish listening, and I swallow down tears. I can't call him back. The things I need to say aren't phone-conversation material, assuming it's a Declan conversation at all. From the beginning, we've kept things focused on the present, rooted in a good time. He's never offered more. I assumed we were taking it one day at a time.

Now, there's a good chance that my future days will be full of new and more horrible cancer treatments. More nausea-inducing drugs and constipating anti-nausea meds. My life will be filled with my family and friends' fear and panic. A few feet away, my mother is tapping away at her phone. She's texting my father, I'm sure. That she didn't call him means that whatever she's saying isn't something she wants me to overhear.

I close my eyes, leaning against the building behind me. My stomach is already sick, thinking about what I dragged them through last year. I'm poised to do it again, and that hurts. It crumbles the beginnings of normalcy I've built over the past month or so.

I don't want to do that to Declan. He's already said that he's not the commitment type. If I'm sick again... I drop my chin to my chest. Will he feel obligated to stick with me, to stay in contact with me? Would he feel guilty calling off a casual relationship with the sick girl?

I won't go through that, not with him.

I was sure, when things started with Declan, that they wouldn't last forever. At most, we had this semester before we went our separate ways, him to the NHL and me into my dream dance career. His path hasn't changed, but mine might. I will not weigh down what's happened between us with any of that.

It's time that I bring things with him to an end.

Declan

IVY DOESN'T CALL ME back. I get a few texts from her, including one where she apologizes for being really busy and unable to talk, but that's it. She decides to stay through the weekend, not making it to the last rehearsal for the opening act she choreographed.

It leaves me with low-level panic in my chest, but I have no idea what to say or ask to get her to tell me what's going on.

She lets me know that she's back on campus on Monday morning, only hours before the final competition. She can't get together before the performance, though, because she's busy putting the finishing touches on the opening dance number. I show up when I'm supposed to, so we can go over the choreography with the rest of the participants again. The dance isn't extremely complicated, and we've practiced two other times.

Her choreographed piece goes off without a hitch. The crowd erupts into applause, exactly as I knew it would. I allow myself to feel some pride for her. She's placed everyone in the proper position, and the overall aesthetic is exactly what we need to kick off the last night of the competition. She worked hard, and it's going to be an excellent addition to her portfolio.

The rest of the eliminated participants go out into the audience to watch, I assume, so it's relatively quiet backstage. We'll go on last, and I hope I'll have a moment alone with her before that, to see how she's doing. But she stays in the dressing room until the third pairing.

I didn't want to jump to conclusions this weekend, but now it's obvious. She's avoiding me.

When we get out on stage, the first strains of our music aren't what I expect. This isn't the song we've been practicing to. The rhythm of it and the beat are the same, but this one's different.

Ivy meets my eyes, then glances away quickly. Did she do this? The show must go on, though, so I start through the first steps of our dance.

I never would have seen myself as a waltzing kind of guy, but even I can appreciate how graceful the dance is. What I can't appreciate, though, is the song choice, "Let It Go" by James Bay. The entire song is about a lover saying goodbye. My eyes meet Ivy's.

What is going on?

Still, we nail the routine, and the entire place goes up in applause. We take our bows. Since we're the last couple, the other four pairs join us on the stage, and we all bow together.

The emcee joins us, full of excitement. "All right, everyone, get your final votes in. We've opened voting, and we're tallying right now. But the window to vote is only fifteen minutes long, so cast your vote right now if you want your opinion to count."

Beside me, Ivy waves and smiles and blows kisses as if she didn't just change everything without telling me. All ten of us file backstage, but I catch her arm, letting everyone return to the dressing rooms without us. "What was that all about? Are you the one who changed the song?"

She lifts one shoulder. "Yeah. I was thinking this morning about how our dances last week were upbeat and optimistic. I thought that artistically, it would make more sense for us to show the range of our ability. So, I changed this one to make it a little more emotional."

I search her face and clench my jaw. I have never been in a position where I've felt the need to look deeper into someone's meaning. I generally take people at face value, but something is wrong here. Ivy's pulling away, and I don't understand why.

"I don't believe that's all. Something feels off between us." I run my hands through my hair, tugging at the strands. "I've barely heard from you all week, and you seem distant. What's going on?"

"I…" Something very much like pain crosses her features.

The emcee interrupts us, waving us toward the curtain. "Dancers," she calls. "We want you guys back on stage. They're going to play some music. Just mess around until we have the final numbers. The organizers don't want the stage to remain empty that long."

I blow out an exasperated breath, and Ivy squares her shoulders, seeming to rally as she squeezes my fingers. "Come on. We're so close. Let's go out and enjoy our win."

I can't return her smile. But I follow her back through the curtain.

The music out here is too loud, so I don't have a second to say anything to her as we wait out the results. I twirl her around, though, as they requested, because I'm supposed to be performing, presenting a good face for the hockey team. After what feels like an eternity, the emcee joins us. She lifts a hand,

and the music stops. It still takes a full thirty seconds for the noise in the place to die down.

They've lit up the seats, too, so I can see the audience now. Earlier, with the lights bright only on the stage, I couldn't tell how many people saw us dance. But now, I can see that the place is packed. There are even signs scattered throughout the sections, cheering on different partners. I don't read them, though, as the emcee starts in.

"First, the performing arts department wants to send out a huge thank you to all of you who came to support our fundraising efforts. The money we raised from this event will be donated in thirds: one to the performing arts department for improvements on this theater, one to the organization whose winning partner is represented, and the last to a local advocacy group that works to beef up representation of the arts in the local community." She waits for the polite applause. "Without further ado, here are your top three pairings. Coming in third place, we have Jackson Taylor, your student body president, and his partner, Olivia McDade, a junior in the dance program." There is thunderous applause. Ivy and I clap along.

"And now, your first runner-up." The emcee pauses for effect. I understand trying to build suspense, but I'm impatient. "Our first runner-up is… football captain, Roman Ellison, and his partner, Dana Tribiano."

The football team on the right side of the auditorium seating explodes into raucous screaming, roaring their approval. Roman takes his bow with Olivia and salutes his crew.

Despite my concerns about what's going on with Ivy, a thrill of excitement races through me. If Roman came in second, then…

"And now, your winners! Let's all give an enormous round of applause to,"—she opens the last envelope and pulls out an index card—"Declan Mitchell, the captain of the hockey team, and his partner, Ivy Devereaux." The noise that follows is deafening, rocking the entire place.

I pick Ivy up and swing her around, reveling in how she feels against me. She laughs, and the sound is triumphant. But as she pulls away and stares up at me, the smile fades from her face. The expression that replaces her joy chills my blood.

I'm right. Something happened with her. I don't know what I did, if it's even me, or if it's something else, but whatever's going on with Ivy is very wrong.

The emcee presents us with one of those huge checks that they always give to the winners of contests. Great media prop. She announces the amount of money that was raised from the event, and even I'm impressed. There's a flurry of pictures. First, we pose with the head of the performing arts department. Then we pose with the director of the athletic department and my coach, who looks supremely uncomfortable in a shirt and tie. After that, we meet the heads of the community advocacy group that will receive the other third of the contribution from the contest. We take pictures with them. By the time all the press finishes, the auditorium has cleared out.

My eyes keep finding Ivy, but each of us is being monopolized in conversation with administration and faculty.

When it appears she might leave without talking with me, I politely excuse myself from my chat with the athletic director, hurry over to her, and place my hand on her arm.

I smile at the group of people surrounding her. "Excuse me for just a moment, please. I would like to speak with my partner for a minute." She makes a polite excuse, and we step away.

I lean closer to Ivy so that we're not overheard. "What is going on? Please don't tell me it's nothing. I didn't hear from you all weekend. You're barely returning my texts, and now it's like you can barely even look at me. Did I do something wrong, something that upset you?" I gently run my hand along her shoulders, and she closes her eyes, something that looks like pain crossing her features.

"No. Nothing like that." She inhales a steadying breath. When she opens her eyes, though, she won't meet my gaze. She gestures to the group she just left. "There are some choreographers here, and a principal for a dance troupe in Philadelphia came to see me. Madame would like me to go out with them, to have a drink. This is a great opportunity for my career. But call me tomorrow, and we'll get together, okay?" She finally makes eye contact. "We'll talk."

There's nothing else for me to say, so I nod.

She squeezes my hand and hurries back to join the group.

As I watch her go, I realize she didn't kiss me goodbye.

Ivy

AFTER STAYING OUT ENTIRELY too late with Madame and the acquaintances she invited to watch my final performance, I get home at almost one and fall into bed without even showering. Exhaustion takes over, and I sleep heavily until almost five in the morning. Then I wake, my body on fire.

My thermometer says I have a low-grade fever, so I take some Tylenol and lie back down, alternately throwing on the covers and kicking them off in my attempts to get comfortable.

In those long minutes, lying in the darkness, I'm plagued by what I can say to Declan when I talk to him later today. There's nothing that is going to make it easy, not for me.

Last night, I could barely look at his face without my heart cracking wide open. He asked me where I was, and the words got stuck in my throat. I want to tell him everything. I want to lay it all out, share it with him, lean on him. But talks about blood tests and imaging are not exactly sexy conversations to have with a guy I'm hooking up with.

He's confused about what's changed. Nothing's changed, but also… everything has. I expected to hear something from Dr. Proctor yesterday. She said that she would probably have results after the weekend. But no calls. It's hard to pretend everything is normal when I'm waiting for the other shoe to drop.

The Tylenol kicks in, and I doze off again. I wake up to the buzzing from the doorbell downstairs. It's Declan.

Stumbling out of bed, I catch sight of my reflection in the mirror behind my door, and I pause. My hair's standing straight up, so I run my fingers through it. I didn't take my makeup off last night. It's all over my face, so I wipe under my eyes, doing my best to get rid of the mascara. Sighing, I accept that it's hopeless. No quick thing is going to fix this mess.

As I hit the button to buzz Declan up, I accept that assessment as accurate to explain me right now too.

I open the door and let him in. He stands right inside the entrance, obviously uncomfortable but looking concerned. "Are you okay?" He glances at the clock. "Did you just get up? It's noon."

I press my hand to my forehead. "It is?" He knows I rarely sleep that late. I was tired last night, but I haven't slept that late in a long time.

"Yeah."

I missed class this morning. *Damn it.* "Well," I begin, trying to get my brain to catch up. "I was out really late with Madame Champion. I guess I just slept in."

"Right." He crosses his arms over his chest. "I thought maybe we could grab some lunch. Are you hungry?"

I'm not, but even if I was, I can't go with him. Not now. I shake my head. "I'm good."

"Ivy,"—his brows drop—"can you do me a favor?"

I nod even as my throat tightens.

"Can you explain to me what's going on in your head right now? Because I'm having a hard time." He buries his hands in his pockets and looks so vulnerable that my stomach heaves.

It's a good thing that I haven't eaten because I'm suddenly very nauseous. "The competition went really well, Declan." I say the words I've planned. I've been practicing them in my head for days, but they still won't come out easily. They're piling up at the back of my throat. "I appreciate how serious you took it. I didn't think you would when we started, as you know. But you proved me wrong." I can't look at him, so I finger the hem of the shirt I fell asleep in last night.

This is awful. But I've done horrible and hard things before. It's best to push through it, rip it off like a Band-Aid. "Now that it's over, I assume we are as well." The words drop between us like a cannonball. There's silence in the aftermath, but the destruction has been done. When he doesn't respond, I continue, "This has been fun. I've had a great time with you. You're a wonderful guy." It's all so vague that it's insulting. I attempt something meaningful. "You made me feel alive for the first time in a long time. You woke me up. I can't thank you enough for that."

"That's what you're going with? Thank you?" His face is tight. "I don't want your fucking thanks."

"Declan…"

He inhales, digging his hands into his head. "Ivy, please… what the hell happened? We were happy. I was happy, anyway, and I thought you were too. What changed? I just… I don't understand."

This is way worse than I could have imagined. I bite my lip to keep it from shaking and take a steadying breath. I'm a performer. I can do this. "You're a playboy, Declan Mitchell.

You said so yourself... you only know how to do casual and that's what this was. Our short-term is over now."

He jerks as if I physically slapped him. His eyes—his beautiful, expressive brown eyes—are roiling with emotions, but he remains silent. I hold his gaze through all of it. Whatever he's feeling, whatever confusion or pain is inside of him, I've caused it. The least I can do is experience it along with him.

Finally, he breaks our gaze and nods. "If that's what you want, Ivy." He steps back, his hand finding the doorknob. "I won't keep you." He meets my eyes again, gives me one of his half grins, and winks. It nearly brings me to my knees. "You take care, okay?"

I can only nod back because I don't trust myself to speak anymore. What I already said was hard enough.

I pull the door closed behind him, then lean against it, in case I drag it open and rush after him. That's what my heart tells me to do. Every part of me is crying out, saying I messed up. I shouldn't push him away.

But hearts are stupid.

This had to happen. If I'm sick, I'm not dragging him through it. He's said he's not cut out for commitment, for anything serious. I'm not going to roll my drama around in his life. It'll be better this way, in the end. He'll move on to someone else, someone who can bring that mischievous smile to his face, someone who will laugh at his sexual innuendos and arch into his touches.

It's for the best for both of us.

Declan

BY THURSDAY NIGHT, I need a distraction. I hit the party at Shepherd hard. We have games this weekend, but they're at home, so I let myself have a handful of shots. I vaguely realize that a couple of girls hit on me, but I have no interest. I leave early, walk home, and fall heavily into my bed. I can only sleep for a few hours, though, before I'm up, rolling around, my brain on autopilot. All I can think of is Ivy's face as she told me she's had a lot of fun with me and thanks me for that while she calls it quits. That's when I roll out of bed.

It's still dark, an hour before dawn, so I put on my sneakers and a hoodie. The walls are closing in on me, so I take a walk.

The February air in northeast Pennsylvania has passed crisp and hit downright freezing. There's frost on the grass, but I stick to the sidewalk, not even sure where I'm going, only focusing on putting one foot in front of the other.

I'm not going to get any more sleep today, so I grab a cup of coffee from a local mom-and-pop shop somewhere in the middle of Chesterboro. I people-watch and take in the sights as everyone starts their mornings. Anything to take my mind off Ivy.

I grab doughnuts for the guys on my way home. None of them are up by the time I open the door, so I put them on the kitchen counter. I don't really want to spend time in my room, and I don't really want to talk to anyone, so I put on workout clothes and head to the rink with my gear. There's probably time for a run before the game, my throbbing, hungover head be damned.

That night, I'm glad for my hockey game. Our game starts at seven o'clock, and I'm there early and ready. While the rest of the guys get dressed, I head out into the corridor with my earbuds and phone. I don't want my weird mood to affect them, so I listen to heavy music, allowing it to pound my senses, and mentally prepare myself to do my pep talks when the team is dressed.

That's when I see my father. I tug my earbuds out, pausing my playlist. Usually, he only makes it to two or three games a season. He's made it to two games in less than a month. This is a record. Maybe hell froze over.

He grins as he joins me. I shake his hand. "Dad, I didn't know you were going to be here today." I glance behind him, but there's no sign of his latest girlfriend. Seeing my father alone feels strange. "Where's Sherry?"

He waves me off. "Oh, I haven't seen her in a couple weeks." He looks me over. "You ready for the game?"

"I guess." I try to muster a smile, but I'm not in a smiling mood.

My father seems to sense that, and his brows drop. It's not like him to address unpleasantness head on. "I was hoping this time that maybe we could go out for dinner,"—he shrugs —"since we didn't get a chance the last time." He leaves unsaid that the reason we didn't get together last time was because he brought some random chick with him.

But there's something almost vulnerable in him, so though I might not have planned to and I'm certainly not excited, I can't say no. "Sure. That sounds great, Dad. I'll meet you down here after the game."

His face splits into a bright grin. "Wonderful. That sounds great. And why don't you invite that girl? The one you didn't introduce me to last time." He glances around as if she's going to appear out of the walls. "I wanted to meet her... whatever girl put that look on your face."

I swallow hard, feeling like my chest is being shredded with knives. "I don't think that's going to be possible. We aren't together anymore." Saying the words out loud is even more painful than hearing them bounce around my head on repeat.

I don't know what flashes across my face, but whatever it is makes my father's mouth tighten. He claps my shoulder through the pad. "I'm really sorry, bud. She looked like a sweet girl. Even though you didn't introduce me." It's as if he couldn't mention her without bringing that up. He shrugs. "Well, from what you've told me, maybe that's for the best. I really think that men like us should stay away from girls who are going to ask for more from us than we're willing to give."

I grit my teeth so tightly that my jaw hurts. "I'm not like you. I can be reliable. That's something that only you can't handle."

My father's face storms over. "Oh, I see. Well, why did you break up?"

"Because she only wanted something casual." I head toward the locker room. I don't need to do this with him right now. I can barely manage my own thoughts. I'm definitely not going to narrate everything to him.

He grabs my arm, his voice low but almost pleading. "Listen, no one ever said you couldn't be reliable. I never said we were the same, but you're the one who's taken steps in my footprints. If you don't want to be the kind of guy who can't keep the good girl, then don't be. We might look the same, but we aren't the same person. You get to choose your own path."

He steps away from me, dropping his arm. "You said your girl wants something casual. If you don't want that, did you say so?" When I don't answer, he snorts. "Here's something I've learned, and you can take my advice or not. Actions speak louder than words, Declan. If you want the girl, tell her so. If she doesn't understand, explain it differently. Make sure she gets it. But after that, if she's willing to give you her trust, be willing to do whatever you have to do to make it work, to prove it to her. She might not want that. Maybe you're right. But you won't know unless you put yourself out there. And if you haven't tried that, then you only have yourself to blame."

He drops his hands. "If she agrees, if she says she's going to give you a chance... then you do whatever you can to hold on to her." He points at me. "I fuck that part up. But you, my boy? You get your own life to fuck up as you choose." He turns and heads toward the stands.

I watch him go, absorbing what might have been the first fatherly lecture he's ever given me.

It can't be that simple. If I go to Ivy and I tell her I love her, put everything on the line, will that actually work? I bury my hands in my hair. Ivy might have been the actual virgin, but I'm the one with no experience where it matters.

I don't know why I didn't do that in the first place. When she called it quits, I didn't object. I should have.

I don't have anything to lose. I've already lost her. When did I become the guy who didn't take risks? If I tell her the truth, at least I'll have tried.

Fired up, I head into the locker room. I rile up the guys, and we hit the ice. I pour my heart and soul into my play. We rack up another decisive victory. We've stretched our lead in our division to four games, and if we keep playing like this, our playoff spot is all but solidified. Afterward, I shoot my dad a text, telling him I'm going to be late because I'm going to see about my girl. He sends back a thumbs up and a fingers-crossed emoji.

I hurry to the Convent, more alive than I've felt in days. I buzz her door, but she doesn't answer. I say into the intercom that I would really like to speak to her. Still no response.

Maybe she isn't home. I pull my phone out of my pocket and drop her a text. Could I please talk to you?

The text bubble appears, then disappears. I wait. Still nothing.

Gritting my teeth, I fold my hands at the back of my neck, staring at the starless sky. This only has a chance if I can get her to listen to me for a minute.

"Hey, Mitch. What are you doing here?" I glance at the sidewalk, where Linc and Shea are walking, hand in hand, toward the Convent.

"Have you guys seen Ivy?" I pull my hands out of my hair. "I just... I really need to talk to her."

They exchange a look but say nothing.

"Well, are you guys going to help me? I can't get in touch with her."

"She went home after classes today," Shea said. "I saw her packing her car up."

"Oh." Well, at least she didn't see me on her intercom and purposely avoid me. I glance at my phone. That doesn't explain why she hasn't texted me back.

Linc puts his hand on her arm. "Shea, you don't know... and she might not..."

Shea shakes her head at him. "Stop. He deserves to know."

"What do I deserve to know?" I ask. I glance between them. "What's going on?"

"She told me she's going home for a doctor's visit."

"A doctor visit? On a weekend?"

"Yeah. She had a lot of stuff with her, almost a carload, so I asked. She said that she might be gone for a little while." Linc steps behind her, folding her in his arms as she continues. "I asked if everything was okay. I know she went through cancer treatment last year. She didn't say anything. Declan, she only shook her head and gave me a hug. She said she'd stay in touch. I don't know exactly what it means."

"Maybe it's nothing," Linc points out.

"Yeah." I nod, my throat tight. "Maybe."

Shea steps forward and wraps her arms around me. She's a small thing, but she's all warmth and a big heart. I let her hug me, and I meet Linc's eyes over her head as the impact of what she said fully hits me.

She's home for a doctor's appointment and might be gone for a while. My heart races, blood pounding in my ears, and my stomach sinks like I'm on a roller coaster.

A doctor's appointment. She didn't tell me that. I have no idea if she knew about this appointment when she broke things off with me on Tuesday, but my gut says she did. If it was only a routine appointment and a weekend trip, she wouldn't have packed her whole car, would she?

What we left unsaid lingers in the air... does this mean that her cancer is back?

I don't know because she didn't tell me. I grit my teeth, staring up at the black sky above us. She told me some about her treatments last year, but there are huge chunks missing. I've gleaned how hard it was on her, how hard it was for her to hold it all together for her family. If she's facing that again, alone... Everything in me hurts right now.

It's clear she didn't think that I could handle whatever she's dealing with... or she didn't think I'd want to.

Shea steps out of my hug, and I give her my best attempt at a grin. "Thanks. If you hear from her, can you please tell her to give me a call?"

"I will." She squeezes my hand, and she and Linc go inside.

Immediately, I pull out my phone and dial her. My call drops into her voicemail, and I clench my jaw. I inhale, then start. "Hey, Princess. I know you said that you wanted things to be temporary and that our short-term is over. But I want you to know..." I pause. "But I want you to know... I don't want a short-term arrangement, and I don't want us to be over. I want you. As much of you as you can give. And I want you to know that I'm willing to give you as much as I have too. If you want me in return." I exhale. "If you do, just please... call me or text me or... anything."

I hang up.

I don't know what is going on in her life or in her head, but I need her to know where I stand. I should have said something sooner.

I can't help thinking, though, that it might already be too late.

Ivy

AS WE WAIT FOR Dr. Proctor to call us back into her office, I stare at the voicemail notification on my phone. It's from Declan. He left it last night, but I haven't been able to bring myself to listen to it. I don't know what he's going to say, but I can't hear his voice, not now. I'm doing my best to be strong. Even hearing him might bring me to my knees.

"Ivy? Mrs. Deveraux?" Dr. Proctor appears in the hallway. "Come with me."

We follow her into her office, and she closes the door behind us.

"I'm so glad that you two could come in on a Saturday. I know it's last minute, but I didn't want to wait any longer." She sits down across the desk from us and rubs her hands together, all smiles. "I know you're eager to find out, so I'll get right to it. We have some good news for you. According to all your test results, we can't find any evidence that your cancer has returned."

I jerk back, sure I misunderstood her. "Excuse me? I'm not sure I heard..."

Dr. Proctor spins her screen so that we can see it, tapping on her keyboard until images pop up. "That's why it took me this long to get to you. I apologize for the delay. I know I said I would have something at the beginning of the week, but I wanted to check with a couple of my colleagues for second opinions." She names two other oncologists. "We all agree. While it's clear that your body is experiencing some sort of immune response to inflammation or infection, we can't find any change in your cancer markers to show further spread. For all intents and purposes, you are still in remission." She beams.

"No cancer," I repeat because it feels like she's talking in a dream. Next to me, my mother clasped her hands together with a squeal, her eyes pinched close.

"Correct. No cancer." Her expression softens. "I'm sure that you both have been concerned this past week, and I sincerely apologize for the delay, but I wanted to make sure that I wasn't making any hasty conclusions."

I nod but can't work up any words. Next to me, my mother is openly weeping.

Dr. Proctor pushes a box of Kleenex across the table to her. Into the silence, she clears her throat and continues. "That's not to say that you are perfectly healthy right now. As we discussed before, your blood counts are not ideal." She pulls up those results again, and we go over the numbers and why they aren't aligning with normal values. "We expect that this is probably the result of some sort of inflammation somewhere else in your body or a virus. In fact, that's why I wanted you to come in today instead of us doing a Zoom call. I'd like to have you tested for mononucleosis."

"Mono?"

"Yes. We tested for EBV antigens and antibodies in your original bloodwork, and we found nothing unusual then. But it's been a couple of weeks. Now, we might be able to detect if there is any evidence to suggest that you have been infected with the Epstein-Barr virus. That's what's responsible for mononucleosis." She shrugs. "There are a few other viruses that could be responsible for mononucleosis as well. We'll look for them too. If it's not that, we'll need to dig a little deeper."

"And it wouldn't have been present in her original bloodwork?" My mom sniffles, but she appears to have regained her composure.

"Exactly. But that would align with your symptoms. Fevers, fatigue, dizziness, and lethargy. Even the night sweat after your fever broke. All of those are symptoms of mononucleosis." Dr. Proctor searches the web, pulling up information about the disease. "As you can see, a lot of the symptoms are very similar to the beginning symptoms of Hodgkin's lymphoma." She inhales. "Let me go over these results with you and explain each of our conclusions. Then we'll talk about where we go from here."

What follows is fifteen minutes of discussion. She goes over all the reasons she and her colleagues believe that I could have this simple virus. "I must impress upon you, though... mononucleosis no joke, and it's certainly not a virus that you should take lightly. You'll need to rest, at least for a while, remain hydrated, and eat well. I'm warning you: you may need to take a little time off from your dancing, at least until your body can recover properly."

"Of course, she can do that," my mother pipes in. "No matter how bad this virus is, it's nothing compared to what we've already been through."

I glance at her, wondering how we are approaching this so much differently. To her, this is just a misunderstanding, nothing to worry about. For me, this entire experience has been a reminder of just how quickly my life can turn around again.

"Let's send you for the tests. We should have those results back quickly, and I'll be able to meet with you later this morning to go over the results."

Mom thanks Dr. Proctor profusely, as if she's directly responsible for my continued remission. Mostly, I listen to them talk, present but also not fully there.

In the waiting room, my mother does a good impression of the Snoopy dance before folding me into her arms in an enormous hug. "Baby, you're still in remission. Did you hear that?"

I pat her on the back. "I did. It's wonderful."

She steps out of my embrace. "What's wrong?"

I drop into one of the seats, pressing my finger against my lips. There's no one here, probably because it's a Saturday and Dr. Proctor rarely has office hours on the weekend. "What if she's wrong, Mom?"

"Baby…"

"No, seriously." I glance up at her. "What if she's wrong? The symptoms… you don't understand. It's almost exactly the same." My eyes bounce around the room. "She and the others think they know. But we should ask her to have someone else look at the results."

"Ivy,"—my mother motions back toward Dr. Proctor's office —"she said she had two other oncologists here to confirm. This is one of the top practices in the city, you know that. One of the best in the tristate area. I'm sure that she's certain."

I bite my thumbnail between my front teeth, my foot tapping. "Yes, but…"

She sits in the chair next to mine and covers my hand with hers. "What's going on?"

I shift in the seat to look at her. "I broke up with Declan."

"Oh, honey, why didn't you say something?" Her eyes fill with concern. "What happened?"

"I thought I had cancer again, Mom." My words are too loud, but I can't seem to control their volume. They burst out of me. "I thought I was sick again, and I didn't want to drag him through it. I didn't want to go through it. I didn't want to put you and Dad through it, and I thought for sure that I was at least saving him from it."

I wave my arm around. "So, my cancer isn't back, at least this time. But is this how it's always going to be? Am I always going to sleep with one eye open, waiting for the worst to happen again? I don't want that, and I definitely don't want that for him." I swallow, but there are tears running down my face. I wasn't even aware that I was crying until they dripped off my chin. "How do I go back to living now after all of that?" The question is raw, ripped right from the heart of me.

With wide eyes, my mother folds me into her embrace. We sit there for long minutes as I openly sob, all great ugly gasps and red face. She rocks me back and forth like she used to when I was a girl and would crawl into her lap when I got hurt. She doesn't mumble any nonsense, though, nothing about how it'll be okay or how it's going to get better. We both know that's not true. Time will pass, and with it, I hope that the immediacy of my fear will fade. But this isn't something that will ever go away. It's something that I will need to learn to live through.

When I finally calm, my mother sifts through her purse and hands me one of the tissues that she must have snagged off Dr.

Proctor's desk. I use it to mop myself up, then take a steadying breath.

"I know you try to hold things together for your father and me. We know you put on a brave face sometimes, when you don't feel it." She wraps her arm around my shoulder. "It's so hard to watch someone you love hurting, physically or emotionally. But loving someone means going through those things with them. It means letting them love you back. It means handing over the hard times, even when they feel like a heavy burden to carry and even when you know you don't want to share them. Caring for people means you risk them hurting you, and you risk hurting them. That doesn't mean that you shouldn't take that risk. If you don't, then you're not really living. You're just alive."

Her own eyes fill, and she dabs at them with another tissue. "Look at us." She shakes her head. "You know what we need?"

"What?" I offer, wiping at my still-dripping eyes.

"We need to get your blood drawn here, and then we need to find a bar and have a drink."

"Mother," I reprimand. "It's ten o'clock in the morning."

"These are extenuating circumstances, baby."

We laugh together and hug again. But when I stand and follow her to the in-office lab, I consider her words.

I was trying to protect her and Dad. I told myself I was doing the same with Declan. But was I really only protecting myself? I pause outside the lab. "Hey, could you go in and just check my paperwork? I wanted to listen to this voicemail."

She cocks her head to the side before nodding. "Sure. But hurry. I'm serious about that drink."

I press play. I'm immediately assaulted by Declan's deep voice, and I press my fingers against my lips. "Hey, Princess."

The nickname steals my breath. He goes on, and when the message ends and I'm alone in the hallway, I stare at my phone, my heart beating wildly in my chest.

His words… they're everything I have wanted with him but was always too afraid to admit to myself. I want him—all of him—but I've never been able to bring myself to ask for that. For all my pretended strength and desire to take chances, I couldn't bring myself to take a risk with my heart. Am I brave enough to change that now?

"Ivy?" My mother pops her head out of the door. "Come on, baby. The faster we do this, the faster we'll have answers."

I nod and follow her inside. His words—those beautiful words—stay with me.

Declan

SATURDAY'S GAME ISN'T AS successful as the night before. We lose 2-1, but we fought hard the whole time. We just couldn't seem to put any pucks in the back of the net. The locker room is somber. The loss breaks a winning streak, and that's always a downer. I do my best to soothe egos, but my head isn't here tonight.

Ivy hasn't called back.

I'm the last one out of the locker room. I take an epic shower, then sit in silence longer than necessary.

When she didn't contact me last night, I had to go to sleep with the sad realization that maybe this isn't something I can fix or that maybe I'm just too late. I thought I was pretty explicit in my message, asking her to give us a real chance. But there were a million other times I should have told her how I felt, and I didn't. That's on me.

I even considered that she didn't get the voicemail or several other reasons she didn't have her phone at all. Except that's stupid. Of course she got the voicemail. She got my message, and she didn't respond. I just need to acknowledge that what I want and what she wants doesn't align.

The rational adult in me understands and accepts that. It happens. But the love-struck idiot who put his heart out there feels pretty beaten up.

I don't regret it. My Dad was right—I'm glad I did it. This is my life, and my choices are my own. I should have taken responsibility for them earlier. Now it's too late.

I stow my equipment and throw my personal stuff into my bag. Zipping my jacket up to my neck, I push out of the locker room and turn off the light. I'll need to put on a brave face at Shepherd, but right now, I'm bone weary, thanks to getting no actual sleep last night. I tuck my hands in my pockets, heading to the exit, my head down.

"Declan."

I shake my head. Now I'm hearing Ivy's voice. I must really be tired. I keep going, but I hear it again.

"Declan. Please. Wait."

I stop, lifting my head. She stands a few feet from the locker room door. She must have been waiting for me, but I didn't see her because I had my head down. To be fair, I wasn't expecting her to be there.

Even as I brace myself, my stomach tilts and my heart picks up. It's so damn good to see her. "Ivy. What are you doing here?"

I probably could have asked that with more finesse, but I'm too tired to pretend right now or be charming. She closes the distance between us with a few steps, and I wish the sight of her didn't hit me like a punch in the center of my chest. This close, though, I notice that her skin is paler. I might regret it, but I can't stop myself. "Ivy... are you sick again?"

A flash of surprise colors her features, but she shakes her head. "No." She pauses. "Well, I am, but I don't have cancer. I have mono." She tilts her head. "Why do you ask?"

I don't answer because I can barely breathe around my relief. My head raises to the fluorescent lighting and my eyes close. Her cancer isn't back. It's mono. Not cancer.

"Declan?"

I rub my sternum, meeting her gaze again. "Yeah?"

"Are you okay?"

I'm sure my smile looks sickly. "Yeah." I swallow. "I thought…" I want to reach for her, but I don't know how she would react, so I bury my hands in the pockets of my jacket. I shake my head. "I'm glad. I mean, not that you have mono. But… you know."

"How did you…"

"Shea." I shrug. "I saw her after the game last night. She said you were packing. That you had an appointment. I was afraid…" I don't expand, because that covers it.

I was afraid.

Ivy shakes her head. "I shouldn't have said anything to her."

"No, I'm sure she wanted to know. She's your friend." I don't know what I am to her anymore. I should have made myself clearer. I should have made her mine. "I'm glad. That's great news."

Her expression closes off. She lifts her phone from her pocket. "Is that why you called me yesterday? Why you left me that voicemail?" I open my mouth, but no words come out. Her lip quivers the slightest bit as she continues. "Did you only say those things because you thought I was sick again?"

I open my arms as if I'm going to reach for her before I stop myself. I drop them fisted to my side. She doesn't need my touch. She needs my words, all the things I should have said to her weeks ago. "God, Ivy. No. I said all of that because I love you." Her eyes widen. "I should have told you sooner, because I think I've loved you from the start. When I'm with you, I feel like I can do anything, like whatever is unsettled in me calms down. I don't want to be without you." I hazard a step closer. She doesn't step away, and that encourages me. "I'm so sorry I didn't say something sooner. I don't know how to be a boyfriend. But I want to be whatever you need, whatever keeps me by your side. I told myself that I was scared I'd hurt you, but really, I'm so afraid that I'm going to screw this up. That I'm going to suck at relationships as bad as my father has. I've watched him let people down my whole life. I can't do that with you, not with something this important."

Ivy searches my face, and I refuse to hide anything. I place my hands on her shoulders, nearly groaning at the feel of her in my hands, when I've spent the past week believing I would never touch her again. "I'm not telling you any of this because I thought you were sick. Last night, when I thought your cancer might be back, all I could think about was that you didn't tell me. You must have been so afraid, but you didn't come to me." I can't let go of that ache, of how much I let her down.

She glances down. "I thought you only wanted something casual. Cancer..." She shakes her head. "That's a heavy burden. I didn't want you to feel like I expected anything from you."

"I want you to expect everything from me. I want to be with you, to be there for you. I want you." I squeeze her shoulders. "Do you want that from me?" I swallow, my mouth suddenly dry. "Do you want me too?"

I hold my breath. Nothing has mattered more to me in my whole life, and I need to know where she stands. Her eyes search mine, and then she reaches for my face, pulling my mouth down to hers. Her kiss holds promise, and it makes me lightheaded. When she retreats, she smiles up at me, her eyes watery. "I love you, Declan Mitchell. So much."

I sweep her into my arm, spinning her around. I bury my face into the crook of her neck, breathing in her lovely vanilla scent, closing my eyes. She laughs, and the sound is music in my ears. My backpack is still on, and we're in a dim and stinky hallway outside the men's hockey locker room, but I can't imagine anything more romantic.

She gasps, jerking away. "Oh my God."

I'm immediately concerned. "What?"

"I just kissed you."

"Yeah..."

"I have mono!" She presses her palms to her cheeks, her eyes wide. "It's the kissing disease. I kissed you. I might have given you mono." She rubs her temples, paling further. "My throat has been sore all week, and I've been exhausted."

I smooth her riotous curls off her forehead, planting a soft kiss on her forehead and then another one on her nose. "Ivy Deveraux, don't you take back that kiss." I punctuate each word with a peck on another part of her face.

"You're in the lead up to playoffs, you idiot." Her brow creases. "You don't have time to be sick."

"Listen here, Princess." I hold her gaze, her face cupped in my hands. "We'll be careful from now on, while you have symptoms. But there is nothing I'd trade for that 'I love you' kiss." I press my forehead to hers. "Nothing."

She closes her eyes, and we stand there like that for a long moment. "I love you, Declan."

"And I love you, pretty girl." I pull away, smiling into her face. "I'm so sorry that it took me so long to say something."

"It wasn't only you." She worries her bottom lip between her teeth. "I believed asking you out was brave, that being with you proved I was ready to live again. But in what really mattered—opening up and sharing myself with you—I was afraid. When I thought I was sick again—" I wait for her to continue. When she doesn't, I squeeze her fingers, and she inhales, meeting my eyes. "I just couldn't see how I was worth the risk. I kept thinking about you watching me be sick and it hurt." She presses the corner of her eye with her knuckle. "I can't promise you that won't be something we face, though. Just to be honest. Most relapses occur in the first three years and my cancer was advanced…"

Her words come fast, a sure sign that she's upset. I shush her. "I refuse to borrow trouble. There aren't guarantees in anything. Not in our careers or our health. But I swear to you —," I squeeze her cold fingers in mine, "—I swear to you I'll do my best to be someone you can depend on. I love you, no matter how hard or easy it is, because being without you isn't an option. I had to consider that this past week. I never want to think about it again."

She throws her arms around me, and I hold her in a crushing grip. When we break apart, I smile down at her. "Let's get out of the locker room hallway."

Ivy casts her gaze around us, at the worn paint on the cinderblock walls, the blue and gray tiles on the floor—the Chesterboro University school colors. "This place is growing on me. It smells like a sweaty armpit, but it has its charms now."

"Does it?"

She grins, and the hope in her eyes nearly brings me to my knees. "It's where we said we loved each other. It's part of our story." I groan, but she pats my arm. "Stop. If we can make this place special, we can do anything."

I hug her to me. "You're right. But right now, lets try somewhere better. Like, somewhere with a bed in it." I wiggle my eyebrows at her, and she laughs.

"I have mono, remember? Transmitted by bodily fluids?"

"There's so much you have to learn, Princess."

Ivy

DECLAN IS TRUE TO his word. When we get back to my room, he showers kisses on every inch of me, being mindful of my sickness. I squirm, begging him to go faster, but he only hushes me and takes his sweet time. By the time he comes inside me, I'm so turned on that I can barely breathe, and when we fall over the edge together, the resulting stillness is bliss.

I fall asleep.

I don't know what time it is when I stir again, but exhaustion still weighs my body down and I'm cold. I twist into Declan's embrace and burrow closer.

"How are you?" He whispers against my hair.

I grunt in response.

"You got feverish. I didn't know if I should wake you up to get you medicine or let you sleep."

That explains why my clothes are damp. I shift to sit. "I'm sorry. Did I wake you?"

His face wrinkles as he studies me. "Stay there." He scurries out of bed, turning on the light on my nightstand. "Which of these drawers has fresh pajamas?"

"I can get them." I move to get up, but he waves me back.

"You're exhausted. Let me take care of you." He points at my dresser. "Which one, love?"

"Bottom one." I fall back on my pillow and close my eyes. "Stupid mono. I haven't been this tired since treatments."

He returns to the bed with a T-shirt and shorts. "These okay?" I scoot up and nod. He helps me out of what I'm wearing and into the fresh pajamas before studying the bed. "Should we change the sheets?"

"I'll get them in the morning." I glance at the clock. Three o'clock. "Well, later this morning." I crawl back under the covers, sighing.

"You said your throat hurt earlier. How is it now?" He scowls. "Maybe we shouldn't have had sex. What if we tired you out too much?"

"Shut it, Mitchell." I close my eyes. "Don't you dare take that back," I say, mimicking him on what he told me after I kissed him last night. "But I would appreciate it if you crawled back in this bed and warmed me up."

His lips tilt, as if he's trying to smother a grin. "Do you need Tylenol?"

"All I need is you right now."

He exhales, but his eyes soften. He sits down, turns off the light, and slides under the covers with me. I sigh, reveling in the warm, bulky heat of him. His arms wrap around me, pulling me closer. We lay in silence for a long moment. I should fall asleep. If I'm going to kick this virus, I need to rest. But for right now, I only want is to be here, awake in the dark with Declan.

"I didn't get to talk to you about your meetings with Philadelphia and Boston." I nuzzle my face into his chest. "I'm sorry. I should have asked about them sooner."

"It's okay." His arms tighten around me. "You can ask me anything you want now." He tucks my head under his chin. "I haven't heard yet, but Howie said that they're watching. He also texted that Seattle called about both me and Linc." I feel his shrug against my ear. "We'll know more the closer we get to playoffs."

"How's our standing?"

"We're favored in our division. But a lot can happen in the next two months. I'm learning to accept that I can only play my roll and lead the best I can. Everything else will need to take care of itself."

"That's very Zen of you."

"We only have so much control." He squeezes me. "You taught me that." I grin, bittersweet tenderness washing over me. "How about you?"

"What?"

"You met a choreographer the night we won the contest. Anything exciting come out of that?"

"Nothing yet." I run my finger along his arm. "I'm supposed to work with Camila Alvarez this week. We wanted to wait until after the first few weeks of school were over before we added in practice." My brow furrows. "Did Ash ever mention her?"

"Camila Alvarez? No. Why do you ask?"

"Because she mentioned him. Said that they dated in high school."

"No. Nothing. But that's interesting."

"Why?"

"I don't know." He considers. "He doesn't hook up. He'll go out and dance, even flirt with girls. But I've never seen him go home with anyone. Doesn't drink much either." I glance up at his face. "Once, when Linc and Shea weren't together yet, he made a comment about how Linc was going to end up fucking it up and regret it forever."

"Well, if the way Camila reacted to his name is any sign, something definitely went wrong between the two of them."

"That's a bummer." We fall into companionable silence. Finally, Declan taps my shoulder. "You should really get some sleep."

"I was actually wondering if we could have sex again."

He bursts out laughing, and then he shifts so fast I can barely see him and tickles me until I'm gasping. Then he replaces his touches with soft caresses, smoothing his fingers along my sides, my arms, my legs. Not one to be outdone, I return the favor. What follows is the most tender lovemaking we've ever had. I allow myself to relearn his body. It's only been a few of weeks since we slept together, before tonight, but so much has happened in that time. As I trail my fingers along his abs, his muscles jump at my touch, and I let the realization that this man is mine sink in. Every gorgeous inch of skin, every sharp gaze, and every quick-witted innuendo. All of his nervous energy and all of his calm. It's all mine to love and treasure.

When I straddle his hips and lower myself on him, I stare down at our bodies. No movement between partners, not any dance, is more beautiful to me than what I see between us here.

He reaches up, smoothing his hand along my shoulder, concern in his eyes. "What's wrong?"

"Nothing." I smile, the weight in my chest heavier and more expansive than any emotion I've ever felt. "Everything is perfect."

Softness like I've never seen washes over his features. Then he clears his throat. "You know what would make this even more perfect?"

"What?"

"If you could move."

I break out into giggles, and he winks at me. This is exactly what's right between us. "I love you, Declan Mitchell."

He swallows, seriousness invading his expression. "And I love you more than I ever thought I could love anyone." His hands squeeze my hips. "Thank you."

"For what?"

"For teaching me about this."

I don't have a good enough response to that, so I lift on my knees and slide back down, taking him deeper inside me. He groans, his eyes closing briefly. But as I fall into a rhythm, he opens them again. Our gaze holds as we move, and the intimacy of it combines with the pleasure, sending me soaring. We come together, and when it's over, I fall on him, completely spent.

I've never felt so content. No matter what life throws at me, with this man on my side, we'll be able to handle anything.

The sleep I fall into is complete and consuming.

Declan

OVER THE NEXT WEEK, I do everything I can to slow Ivy down and make sure she gets well. It's a lot harder than I expect it to be. She doesn't relax well. Not that I'm one to talk. I probably wouldn't be a good patient either. We're athletes. Not being able to move would just feel wrong.

I do what I can, though. Mostly I coax her to snuggle on the couch, watching movies. I bring her food, so she doesn't have to go anywhere but to class. I make sure that she gets to sleep early. She complains, but I have my methods to keep her happy.

By Friday night's game, she's improved enough that she refuses to stay away from the rink. I talk her into a nap, though, and her cheeks are pink by the time I leave her to go to the game. She seems to improve. Every day she can stay awake a little longer, go a little further without tiring out.

After I run through my pre-game conversations with the guys, I meet Ivy in the hallway. She's wearing my away jersey. If I didn't know she had mono, I'd assume she was any other happy co-ed. She's the picture of health.

And she's all mine.

I fold her against me, and she laughs, even as she wrinkles her nose at my smelly equipment. I hold her closer as I catch sight of someone over her head. I take a deep breath and smile at him.

"Hey," I say, drawing back. "There's someone I hoped you would meet." I wave my father over. "Ivy Deveraux, this is my father, Harvey Lowe." I tuck her against my side. "Dad, this is my Ivy."

My dad sticks out his hand to her. "Hello, Ivy," he offers her a charming grin. "It's nice to finally meet you." He gives me a shove. "It seems my son has been keeping me away from you."

"Dad…" I start, immediately wary. "It's not like that."

"Actually, sir." Ivy laces her arm in his. "He could want to keep me away from you." She drops her voice to a whisper. "I'm a bit of a bad influence."

My dad sputters a laugh, patting her hand. Then he winks at me. "I like this one, Declan."

I extricate my girl from his grasp, tugging her back against my side. "I do, too, Dad."

"I'm going to find my seat," my father says, grinning at us. "But I'd love to take you out after the game. Both of you." He squeezes our arms.

"Ivy's been sick…" I start, but she cuts me off.

"I'd love that, Mr. Lowe," she finishes, casting me a dirty look.

"Harvey. Please."

"Of course, sir," she nods.

He chuckles and waves, heading toward the bleachers. When he's out of sight, I glance down at her. "Are you sure? You're still not one hundred percent. I don't want you to wear yourself out."

"You can't keep him from me," she offers softly. "I know that you two have a strained relationship, but I want to know all of you. That means knowing him, too."

I nod but can't speak around the lump in my throat. This week with her has been nothing short of magic. Her love and acceptance humble me every day.

The team joins me in the hallway, all nervous energy, as they run through their pre-game preparations. There's swinging arms and pacing. I lean down and kiss Ivy on the cheek. We're still avoiding mouth to mouth contact, thanks to her virus. She hugs me again before she turns. I snag her arm.

"Aren't you going the wrong way?" I ask. "I thought you said you were going to sit in the spectator section with Cami?"

This past week, Ivy and Cami Alvarez have really hit it off. They've had a few different choreography sessions, and Ivy has raved about her passion for her work and her sunny disposition.

Ivy shakes her head. "She texted me a couple of hours ago. Judd Jones is coming into town to see her. She asked if it would be okay if she came to the game with him instead."

"Judd Jones?" I attempt to place the name. "That sounds familiar…"

"He starred in the latest superhero movie, the one with Robert Downey, Jr."

"Oh, right." I smile. "He's pretty famous."

Ivy shrugs. "I guess they're dating or something."

"Wait," Ash offers over my shoulder. I didn't even realize he was there. "Did you say that Cami Alvarez is dating Judd Jones?" His face has paled. "The actor?"

Ivy glances between us. "I mean, she didn't say for sure…"

"But he came here, specifically to see her?"

"Well," she looks at me helplessly. "I guess so. Yes."

His jaw firms and he nods before stepping forward, to the front of the line, waiting to go out.

"I'm sorry." Ivy lifts her hands, her voice hushed. "I didn't realize..."

"I don't even know what's going on," I assure her. "But whatever is between Cami and Ash is theirs to work out. It has nothing to do with you."

"I know." She sighs. "I like them both, though. I hope they sort it out."

I tug her closer, hating to see even this much sadness on her face. "Now why don't you find your way to my seat." I lean closer, nuzzling her ear. "By the way, have I told you how good you look in my clothes?"

She leans up and whispers, "As good as I look without clothes on?"

I pretend to consider. "I wouldn't go that far…"

Her laugh sends happiness lacing through me, and I smile too, unable to stop myself. "Now hurry. We're about to go out." She nods, squeezing my hand. "And Ivy?" She glances back at me. "I love you."

She opens her mouth to respond, but the guys are all around and they break out in obnoxious catcalling. Some of them make kissing faces, shoving me playfully. "Shut up, you assholes," I say, but there's no heat to it. I don't care what they think, not with the happiness in her eyes and that smile on her lips.

When they quiet down, she clears her throat. Then she says loud enough that it echoes through the hallway, "I love you, too, Declan Mitchell."

I wink at her, and she flounces out of the tunnel toward my seat. The guys whoop it up, showing her their appreciation. As we make our way out onto the rink, with my girl's eyes on me and the smell of the ice in my nose, I can't imagine my life being any better than it is right now.

About Author

Josie Blake writes college-set, hockey romance with sass and emotion. She also writes award-winning romantic suspense and scifi thrillers as Marnee Blake.

Originally from a small town in western Pennsylvania, she now battles traffic in southern New Jersey where she lives with her hero husband and their happily-ever-after: two very energetic sons. When she isn't writing, she can be found next to a hockey rink or swimming pool, cooking up something sweet, or hiding from encroaching dust bunnies with a book. She loves to hear from readers so please feel free to drop her a note or visit her website at josieblake.com. Connect with her on Instagram at instagram.com/josieblakeauthor, or on Facebook at Facebook.com/JosieBlakeAuthor

23309470R00143